Praise for Vivian Arend's
Turn It Up

"This is definitely another one of my favorite Vivian Arend books. It had it all: heat and explicitness, pace, tropes I love and main characters I totally clicked with, a hero who shot to the top of my favorites list and last but not least the right amount of back-story and secondary stuff to create a perfect balance. Thank you, Ms. Arend for once again keeping me entertained and for never disappointing me when I open one of your books to read."

~ *Pearl's World of Romance*

"I enjoyed every aspect of this book. The chemistry was off the charts from the very beginning... This is one of those feel-good books that I know I'll be going back to time and again."

~ *Novel Thoughts*

"I enjoyed Ms. Arend's voice and writing style thoroughly. If you like a relationship driven story, that encompasses two of my favorite themes, friends to lovers and a May/September romance, you may like to give *Turn It Up* a try."

~ *Book Lovers Inc.*

Look for these titles by
Vivian Arend

Now Available:

Xtreme Adventures
Falling, Freestyle
Rising, Freestyle

Granite Lake Wolves
Wolf Signs
Wolf Flight
Wolf Games
Wolf Tracks

Forces of Nature
Tidal Wave
Whirlpool

Turner Twins
Turn It On
Turn It Up

Pacific Passion
Stormchild
Stormy Seduction
Silent Storm

Six Pack Ranch
Rocky Mountain Heat
Rocky Mountain Haven

Bandicoot Cove
Paradise Found
Exotic Indulgence

Takhini Wolves
Black Gold

Print Collections
Under the Northern Lights
Under the Midnight Sun
Breaking Waves

Turn It Up

Vivian Arend

SAMHAIN
PUBLISHING

Samhain Publishing, Ltd.
11821 Mason Montgomery Road, 4B
Cincinnati, OH 45249
www.samhainpublishing.com

Editing by Anne Scott
Cover by Angie Waters

First Samhain Publishing, Ltd. electronic publication: February 2011
First Samhain Publishing, Ltd. print publication: January 2012

Dedication

Turn It Up is book number ten for me with Samhain Publishing. Not sure if this is considered a dedication, or just a heartfelt thank you.

Hurrah to Laurie, for giving me a chance in the first place. Cheers to Crissy, who runs a damn fine show. Lindsey, Amanda, Marty, Tina, Jacob and Jimmy, who keep the behind-the-scenes action flowing smoothly, you are all gold.

But most of all, to Anne Scott, who doesn't let me take it easy and puts up with more missing commas than any editor should have to. I'm so glad I get to work with you. Here's looking forward to the next ten...or more.

(Note the casual way I slipped a set of ellipses into that last sentence, for remembrance.)

Chapter One

The doors of the Sugar Shack swung shut behind her and Natasha Bellingham drew a sigh of relief, thankful to get out of the blinding morning sunshine. Her body hurt all over and she could have sworn she had a slight headache, but her brain was too numb to be sure.

A deep chuckle rose from her right, and she twisted slowly to stare into Maxwell Turner's grinning face. She closed her eyes and struggled to stay on her feet. "Oh damn, you're here already."

A hand slid around her waist and she peeled her eyes open as he guided her to an overstuffed chair in the farthest corner of the café. It happened to be the darkest corner as well, shaded from the bright light pouring in the floor-to-ceiling windows. He seated her and held out a glass of water. She gulped it gratefully.

Now if he'd wipe that silly grin off his face, she might consider thanking him, even if it was an ungodly hour. It took way too much effort to check her watch. The numbers blurred before her, but it had to be well before her intended wake-up time of two in the afternoon. This was far too early to be up the morning after her final big bender.

"I'll grab us coffee. I assume you don't want anything to go with it."

Flashing her middle finger was tempting, but that would have required more energy than she currently possessed. He laughed again and strode away, his ass flexing nicely under his worn jeans. Not that she noticed. She'd sworn years ago not to notice anything sexual about him.

She sighed. Even with her head the size of a football, there was no escaping the truth. He'd grown into a good-looking man. She still wasn't interested.

Liar.

Tasha leaned back on the comfortable high-winged chair and breathed slowly. Maybe if she didn't move for a week her head would return to normal. The café was peaceful, people chatting quietly, wonderful smells of dark roast drifting on the air.

"Coffee, double double, on the table at six o'clock. Drink up, we'll talk once you've found peace with the universe."

"Oh, you're funny." Her head might split in two if she laughed, or she would have been more amused.

He sat opposite her, face in profile. She picked up her coffee and sucked down the liquid with a vengeance, attempting to kill the aftereffects of a few too many drinks.

Few? Last night had been all about taking it to the limit. She never drank that much, ever. Her head hurt. Even her eyelashes were way too heavy.

The steaming fluid slid down her throat, and she relaxed deeper into her chair, letting it cradle her. Movement caught her eye as Maxwell stretched out his legs and leaned back, and she casually took stock. Faded jeans, slightly scuffed at the knees, white button-down shirt. The edge of a pale-blue T-shirt peeked from the open neckline. He'd cut his dark hair shorter than usual sometime in the past week. The style suited him. Made him look older than the baby of twenty-four she knew him to be.

At the table to their right, a couple of young women openly admired Max, and Tasha forced herself to relax. When the girls glanced in her direction then tucked their heads together to whisper, she recited a few calming mantras. This was definitely not a good morning. She was tired, cranky, and there wasn't enough caffeine in all of Thompson to deal with the headache she would have when the rest of the alcohol faded from her system.

She returned her cup to the table and rested her chin in her palm, leaning heavily on an elbow. The smooth surface was cool under her elbow and she covered a yawn. Oh yeah, the coffee needed to kick in fast. Max turned to face her squarely, one hand wrapped around his mug.

Tasha cleared her throat. "I'm confused. My alarm, that I swear I didn't set, went off this morning. Very early this morning. Then the phone rang—you—leaving a message reminding me to show up on time." She paused. Admitting she had no idea what was going on was embarrassing. "I don't remember arranging to meet today. Did we really plan to get together?"

He nodded. "I assume you took a cab?"

As if she would drive. She was probably still over the legal limit. "Of course. Look, I'm sure there's a fabulous reason why we need to chat, but I'd appreciate if we could switch to tomorrow. I was out kind of late last night."

"I know."

She growled at him but stopped when the sound made her brain ache. "Then you should understand I don't want to be vertical."

The flash in his eyes as he looked her up and down did silly things to her system. "You don't have to be. If you'd like me to

11

get you horizontal, I'm all for it."

An instant shot of lust raced through her and she mentally beat it into submission. "Stop that."

He shrugged innocently and sipped his coffee again, ignoring her orders to stop flirting, just like always. When in hell had she lost control of him? "I'm not changing my mind. I will not date you, so if you're hoping to catch me in a moment of weakness..."

"Weakness, like when you're completely hungover from tying one on? Happy birthday, by the way. I have a present for you, but I'm not giving it over until you're sober."

"Bastard."

He tsked softly. "Now now, that's not true. My mom and dad were married when I was conceived. Although I'm not sure about my sister."

Her head spun. For as long as she'd known him, he'd spoken in riddles. Usually she found it hilarious, watching others sputter and try to figure out what he meant, but at the moment, when she wasn't at her best, she understood why people found him annoying.

"You're twins."

"Right. Good to know you're a little more with it than you were last night."

She stared at him in confusion. "Last night? You weren't there."

"Sure I was. I was the DD for the evening. Or don't you remember Lila calling me? By the time you'd all done a round or four of tequila shooters, you'd talked her into drinking as well, and there was no one left sober enough to get behind the wheel."

"You drove us home?"

"Every last one of you."

Natasha drained her mug and stared at the bottom, wondering if she dared have another. She needed to be alert to keep up with Max. She had no recollection of him driving her anywhere. There had been lots of singing, that she remembered, but him?

The tease of another cup of the Sugar Shack's high-test java tempted her. If she stuck to her schedule, this was her last day for coffee as well.

Max held out his hand. "A dying man's final requests are always honored. You're going to feel like hell for a few days anyway, you may as well enjoy the buzz while you can."

She handed over her cup reluctantly. He seemed to know *way* too much about what she had planned.

He strolled back to the counter and got her a refill while she racked her brains for an inkling of what had happened last night. She remembered hitting the bar with her friend Maxilila and a few other girls. Her birthday was as good a time as any for one last hurrah before cleaning up her act and going dry for as long as it took.

Operation Baby—before that magic number of thirty-five hit and she turned into a pumpkin or something.

She'd always hated the cliché of the damn clock ticking, but over the past couple of years that was exactly what she'd heard. Every month as the dream of starting a family seemed to grow more distant, the timer counting down got louder and louder.

Sunlight flashed off the tabletop and she groaned in pain as her temples throbbed in response. Of course, right now the thought of being responsible for anyone other than herself scared her silly. She should crawl back into bed and sleep until Monday.

It was a brilliant plan, and one she was going to put into action as soon as possible. But first, she had to ditch Maxwell.

Max added extra cream and sugar to Tasha's coffee cup. It was unlikely she would be eating anything soon, and at least this way she'd consume a few calories. He nodded at the barista and picked up their cups, balancing them easily as he returned to the table.

She'd leaned back in the oversized chair, head resting against the side wing. In contrast to her dark hair, her skin was pale, and she must have had a headache the size of California. But he wasn't about to let this chance slip away. For the past four years he'd been biding his time. He recognized an opportunity when he saw one, and this was it—Natasha Bellingham was going to be his. Enough of her running, and if he had to take advantage of the moment, so be it.

Her nose twitched when he placed the cup in front of her and he laughed. "I don't understand how you think you're going to survive without coffee. You're pretty near addicted to the stuff."

She narrowed her eyes, the dark brown irises locking on him. "That's the second time you mentioned that, about me giving up coffee. How do you know what I've got planned?"

"You told me." He gave her a serious nod, keeping all traces of amusement hidden. "Last night, when I helped you up to your apartment."

"You helped me..." Her eyes clouded over for a moment. She shook her head, then cringed. She sucked back more of her coffee and he let his smile escape.

"There were a number of interesting revelations last night. How you weren't embarrassed about having a good time with your friends because it was your last time drinking for as long as it takes. And then there's the coffee you're giving up—as well as any kind of tea but herbal."

Two red circles appeared on her cheeks and she stuttered. One deep breath later, Max watched in amazement as she turned calm and cool before him, the embarrassed, hungover woman vanishing beneath a perfectly in-control persona.

"Well, it appears you've found out about my new health régime. Part of getting older. Time to take care of the body a little better."

Damn, she was good. If he didn't know her so well, he would have fallen for the cool, collected and put-together routine she displayed.

She leaned forward and stared at him intently. "Was there something specific you wanted? The message on my answering machine mentioned a business proposal."

"That's right."

He tipped back a hit of his coffee, trying to waste a few minutes. Fortunately, last night the calm woman before him had been far more hot-blooded and emotional. He wouldn't hold it over her head, but he would capitalize on what she'd let slip.

As he waited for her breathing to fall back into a steady pattern, he pulled out the file folder he'd prepared after tucking her into bed last night—and he wasn't about to tell her that part either. Not yet. Even though the memory of her soft skin made him instantly aching and hard, he had forced himself to not take advantage of the opportunity.

It had nearly killed him to slip her under her quilt and not crawl in with her. Especially after listening to her confess what she wanted, what he was more than willing to provide. If he hadn't been raised to be a gentleman, it would have made life so much easier. Giving in and fucking her while she was drunk was no way to start a lasting relationship.

15

He handed over the portfolio.

Tasha accepted it with reluctance, pulling it toward her. "What's this? I'm not up for any games today, okay?"

He shook his head. "No games. Take your time, read it through."

She rubbed her eyes for a moment then opened the file with a deep sigh. Humoring him no doubt. Her gaze darted over the page and slowly her brow furrowed.

"Maxwell, I think you gave me the wrong papers. These are your health records."

He smiled. "That's right. I had a full physical last month and all the paper work is up to date. I thought you'd appreciate that."

She snorted. "Oh yeah. Thank you. Exactly what I need to see the night after I drink myself shit-faced. Good for you." She scrolled down the page with a finger. "Gee, nice blood pressure. And your BMI is amazing. You should be proud."

Max chuckled. "Ahh, I love your sense of humor."

Tasha leaned back and sighed. "Look, I don't feel well. Get to the point. I know you're smarter than anyone else, so use small words and I'll try to understand."

"Turn the page. I think you'll get the picture."

She rolled her eyes then winced in pain, and he wiped his mouth to hide his grin. While he felt for her, he was grateful the liquor last night had been enough to loosen her lips. At least enough to make her spill the beans in regards to her plan to get pregnant.

Which fit his agenda just fine.

She turned the page and froze, her mouth hanging open as she stared at the open file before her. The twin spots of color on her cheeks spread to flush her entire face, and she slammed her lips together.

He waited. He was good at waiting.

"Maxwell Dale Turner, what the hell is this?"

Tasha flipped the portfolio around to display the ring he'd taped to the page below the note written in all capital letters.

WILL YOU MARRY ME?

Chapter Two

The constant pulse of blood through her temples was louder now than when she'd arrived at the coffee shop. And if Junior didn't stop grinning and start talking, she was going to remove his tonsils with a spoon.

"I think it's pretty clear. I didn't even use fancy words. Plain and simple, like you requested." He motioned to the file. "Go on, read it."

She stared at the silver ring. It shone against the stark white background of the paper. Maxwell's neat handwriting continued below where it hung.

In light of your desire to start a family it seems—

An icy chill washed over her as she tore her gaze from the page to stare at him. "How did you find out I wanted to start a family?"

She hadn't told anyone. Not her closest friend, not *anyone*.

"You told me. Last night. While you were getting undressed you—"

Getting undressed? She snapped up a hand and he stopped dead in mid-sentence. Conversations continued to float around them, light laughter carrying from a few tables over. The whole situation was surreal and this was not the place she wanted to hold this discussion. Not where they could be overheard.

Because it sounded like they had a few things to discuss.

"Drive me home," she demanded.

He stood and held out his hand. If she could have made it out the door without wavering, she would have ignored the offer, but ending up on her ass on the floor would be more traumatic than accepting his assistance. They walked outside in silence where she paused to root in her purse for her sunglasses.

Max opened his car door and she slid onto the leather seat. The dark-toned interior and shaded windows eased her pain a little. He squatted beside her, leaning across her body to fasten her seatbelt. The spicy scent of his aftershave made her mouth water as her face settled into the crook of his neck.

She pushed him away, trying to hide her reaction. "I can do that."

He seemed to slow deliberately, his hands lingering over the strap, and her pulse leapt up another notch. "I know you can, but I want to help. Relax. I'll take you home, then we can talk."

Tasha rubbed her temples as he closed the door and strode around to the driver's side. Head held high, shoulders back. His arms looked thicker than she remembered, and she wondered if he'd been working out or something.

Dammit, no, she didn't wonder. She wasn't ogling his body and she was completely uncurious why he had the audacity to propose. What she needed to concentrate on was last night. On him taking her home and what other secrets she might have spilled. Obviously her idea to have a drink or two as a last hurrah had backfired in more than one way. Now she felt like hell *and* had a major problem to deal with.

Maxwell Turner had been pursuing her for years. From the

moment he'd issued his first ridiculous invitation as a boy of seventeen, she'd made it blatantly clear she wasn't interested. Yeah, she'd lied her ass off, at least about not being physically attracted to him, especially as he got older. Still, there was no way she was getting involved with him. Her friend's *much* younger cousin? Damn, if the guys she'd been dating couldn't act like grown-ups and keep their dicks in their pants, what could she expect from a pup?

She was done with cheating, lying, out-to-get-what-they-wanted men. She didn't need them, not for anything. Spending time with Maxwell as a friend—especially around the Turner clan—that was doable. He was a decent-enough fellow, as long as they didn't get romantically involved. Anything more? She wasn't stupid enough to fall into the dating trap again.

He drove slowly, windows rolled down. The fresh fall air drifted in, cooling her feverish skin. Light rock music played softly, and she closed her eyes. She needed five minutes respite before figuring out how to deal with this insane situation.

A slight motion rocked her and she sat upright with a jerk. She must have fallen into a doze—half asleep, half still drunk. Maybe Max would agree to call off the rest of the morning, and they could pick this up in the future once she'd gotten her brain back.

Tasha fumbled for the seat-belt release as he opened her door. She didn't need his hands on her again, thank you very much. She was committed to this path. No men in her life. No more having to defend her heart. Just because her body reacted didn't mean she had to give in.

She did accept his hand out of the vehicle, only to stop in confusion. "Why are we...? Max, you brought me to my building site. I asked you to take me home."

"And I will. But this is one of your homes, so strictly

speaking I did what you asked."

His grin was back and the urge to smack him one grew larger by the minute. "You are so annoying."

Maxwell opened the trunk and pulled out two lawn chairs. "Come on, let's talk."

She followed behind as he paced toward the skeleton frame of what would eventually be her home. After years of working for other people, she'd finally gotten the chance to take her own dreams and put them down on paper. The architectural designs she'd created were slowly being turned into a reality. The foundation was poured, the weeping tile and backfill completed. The framers were hard at it this week with most of the outer walls up and the sheeting beginning to close it in so it actually looked like a house.

He unfolded the lawn chairs in the future living room and gestured to one. She shook her head. Standing would be better, especially when he arranged his long limbs into one chair. That allowed her to get the upper hand, right? Being taller than him for once?

"What did I tell you?" she blurted out. Oh, that was controlled and dignified. *Not.* He raised a brow and grinned wider, and she bit back a smart comment. "I mean, tell me what happened last night, please."

Max crossed his ankles and placed his elbows on the armrests, looking entirely too relaxed and comfortable. He wasn't suffering nearly as much as she was.

"You explained to me how stupid men were, and I had to agree since you were discussing the idiots you've dated over the past couple of years. Then you informed me this being the modern world there was no reason for you to try to find a Prince Charming." He made quote-unquote motions with his fingers, his dark eyes fixed on hers as he spoke. "I agreed with you on that one as well, in case you're interested."

"I thought you liked to argue with me."

"Only when you're wrong. Most of your revelations last night were amazingly accurate."

She dragged the second lawn chair farther from him and collapsed into it. "Last night... Umm, what else did I say? Or do? Because I was too drunk for you to think I was serious. It must have been the alcohol talking."

He tapped his fingers together as he considered. "No, the alcohol-influenced bit came when you stripped off your clothes right after we walked in the door."

Dear Lord, no. "You're kidding me."

Maxwell took a deep breath. "There's no easy way to say this, so I'll simply spit it out. Three sheets to the wind, you're very chatty. You're also very affectionate. Don't worry, nothing physical happened between us. I carried you to your room, convinced you to put on your PJs and tucked you into bed. I did not accept your offer to fuck your brains out."

Tasha opened her mouth but her vocal cords were frozen. She couldn't have. Max dragged his chair back to its original distance from hers and grabbed her hand. His thumb traced slow circles on her knuckles, and that flutter of desire she'd kicked into the corner years ago woke up and stretched.

He spoke quietly, the deep tone smoothing over her skin like butter on hot toast. "You insisted you were not usually a drunk, and that's true. I've never seen you lose control like that ever before."

"And never will again." God, she was so embarrassed. A tingling sensation stole up her arm from where he caressed her skin. He'd flipped her hand over to rub the tender inside of her wrist and tendrils of desire flew along her nerves.

She pulled her fingers free. "Stop that."

He shrugged and leaned back, crossing his arms over his chest. Yup, definitely larger muscles—broader across the... *No. No admiring the man.* She had to get to the bottom of this puzzle so the insanity could be finished.

"Max..."

"You told me about Operation Baby."

Tasha sucked for air. "No. Way."

"Yup. No time like the present, there are plenty of opportunities for a woman like you to successfully raise a child alone. Damn if you'll wait any longer for the right guy to come along. Artificial insemination will work fine."

She buried her head in her hands with a moan as he repeated verbatim all the arguments she'd had with herself over the past year. *Shit, shit, shit.* She'd told him everything, while naked to boot. What the hell had come over her, and how could she possibly explain this away? Her face flamed red hot with embarrassment.

Confusion flooded her already overtaxed brain and she stared at him in dismay. No matter how dense she'd been, that still didn't explain the ring he'd offered.

"Let me get this straight. I stripped in front of you and told you my plans for getting pregnant before I turned thirty-five. Your response was to set my alarm clock, give me your health records and *propose*?" Tasha scrubbed her temples in frustration. This was not happening. She grabbed the armrests of the lawn chair so tightly they creaked. "Junior, I may be a stupid drunk, but what's your excuse? You were sober and you're acting more insane than me."

"You've rebuffed me for a long time." His dark eyes caught hers, locking her in place. A wave of his hair fell across his brow, hanging untended as he gazed intently at her. "Now that

23

I've finally found something I can give you, I wanted to be sure you listened."

"That you can give me... Wait a minute." *No. Freaking. Way.* He was nuts. "Your health records? Are you offering stud services to get me pregnant? Because, buddy, that's—"

He laughed and the lightness of it danced around the room, filling the open spaces with the sound of his delight. "I'm offering more, but that's a damn good place to begin. You think you're getting old enough you need to start a family immediately. Personally, I don't think there's any rush, but if it's that important to you, fine. But artificial insemination? Why would you go with an anonymous donor? No matter how good the charts, you've got no guarantees. I, on the other hand, can provide complete health records, plus a family history with no inherent health risks. Long-lived grandparents, and a decent chance at a fantastically attractive kid." Max waggled his brows and she groaned.

He was serious. Tasha shot to her feet, ignoring the stabbing pain it caused, and paced away from him. Her fingers twitched with the need to shred something.

"You forgot to mention the streak of insanity that shows up every now and again. Maxwell, you *proposed* to me. Now you're offering to get me pregnant? Maybe I'm still too hungover to connect all the dots, but none of this makes sense."

"You want the long version or the short?"

"Short, dammit," she snapped. "Give me the short list and be done with it already."

Max let out the breath he didn't realize he'd been holding. Surely if she was going to tell him to fuck himself, she would have by now. If she'd been completely uninterested, she could have cut him off back at the café. Ordered her own cab, or done something to stop their discussion from continuing. He grabbed at the chance to state his case.

"A list? You got it. Short, to the point. Number one, you want a baby. Two, you think the world of my family. Three, you said once a long-term relationship should be a matter of choice, not some emotional bleeding-heart impulse or sexually hormone-driven whim."

She snorted. "Your freaky perfect memory's going to get you in trouble someday."

"I'm waiting in breathless anticipation. Am I right? Did I hit three truths in the short list?"

Her gaze narrowed as she nodded. "Why do I feel like I'm being set up?"

"Because you're nearly as smart as me?" Tasha gave him the finger and he grinned. "Look, maybe I'm a bit out of line, but we've been friends for a long time. You've hung out with the Turner clan for years and gone to all kinds of family events with me around. I'm going to speak bluntly, okay?"

"And you don't usually?"

"No, I'm far too polite and laid back."

"Oh, *Jesus*, just get on with it."

He rose to his feet and closed in on her. "I think if it's at all possible, all babies should have both a mom and a dad to love and care for them."

"If possible," she retorted. "I'm single."

"Not if we get married."

She dragged her hands through her hair. "This isn't happening. I swear it's some kind of tequila-induced hallucination."

He stepped closer, not giving her time to continue her protests. Last night he'd shown more control than any man should ever have to. Today his ability to manage the urges driving him grew a little shakier. "My family thinks the world of you and would be thrilled to be involved with your child—again meaning more love and attention. That's not the biggest reason to marry me, but it's a bonus."

"Like a prize in the cereal box?"

Max laughed out loud, the expression on her face driving him crazy. Sarcastic wench. "God, you are so freaking cocky. I love that. And that's the real reason this makes sense. I would definitely choose to be in a long-term relationship with you."

She opened her mouth to speak then swung her hands in frustration, pacing away to stand in front of an empty window opening. Fists planted on her hips, she stared out at the backyard.

He waited patiently.

Tasha turned and shook her head. "You can't know that. You're too young to—"

"Don't." That was the one argument he would not accept. It made his blood boil. He rapidly crossed the room to her side. "Don't you dare say something trite like 'You're too young to know your own mind.' This is *me*, not some random person off the street. We've spent tons of time together over the years."

"Not one-on-one, not in a sexual relationship."

"Because you've never let us go there. I've been your friend. I've helped you move and fixed your car. We've played games together and watched bad movies. When I make a decision I stick to it. If I say I want to be involved with you, trust me, I've given it a ton of thought. I'll not only keep my commitment, but be the best damn father possible."

Her face grew redder as she waved her hands in the air and shouted at him, "You can't propose to me just because I want to get pregnant."

It was his turn to stare in disbelief. "This from a woman who *plans* on making a baby and having to deal with wet diapers and colic and all the rest of it alone for the next twenty years? Don't talk to me like I'm the only crazy person in the room."

They locked glares, neither one blinking or willing to back down. The wind picked up and blew in the open window, ruffling her hair around her face and something inside him tightened. Was he in love with her? Hell, yeah. He'd admired her forever, her body and her character, and love seemed to have snuck in as a natural progression, but that's not what she needed to hear, not yet. She'd spent too long keeping him at arm's length. He'd have to start somewhere they could agree. Max took a step closer, dropping his gaze to her lips. She licked them nervously, crossing her arms in front.

"What are you doing?" She shuffled backward, coming to a sudden stop against the raw wood of a two-by-six wall stud, flinging her hands out to catch her balance.

"Proving we've got a physical attraction between us." One more pace put him in her personal space, their feet alternating on the floor, torsos brushing, hips close enough the heat of her body bled against his.

She leaned harder against the wood at her back, her breasts heaving beneath her T-shirt as she tried to widen the space between them, and he refused to give way. "What does that have to do— I mean, I'm not sure what you're talking about."

Max sank his fingers into her thick mane of dark hair and let his satisfaction escape in a low moan. God, he'd wanted to do that forever, and last night refusing her sexual advances had taken him to the breaking point. He needed this so badly he felt raw inside, aching with need for a taste of her. He tugged until her face tilted toward him, the smooth curve of her cheek shining in the midmorning sunlight. "Just in case you get some screwy idea of accepting only part of my terms. I don't want you to imagine for even a moment we're going to use any kind of turkey-baster method to get you pregnant."

Her eyes widened and she opened her mouth, probably to lambaste him. He took advantage of the opportunity and clamped their mouths together.

Chapter Three

Stone cold sober.

Suddenly, that's what she was—the blood pounding through her carrying more than enough oxygen to reinvigorate her dusty brain cells. He was kissing her. No, that was wrong. A kiss was something your granny gave you, something innocent and calm that made you slightly sleepy. This was a different beast altogether, like a flash fire rolling through and consuming everything in its path, and before she realized what she was doing, Tasha had wholeheartedly joined in.

Maxwell Turner wasn't only kissing her, he had his body so tight against hers there was no doubt remaining that various parts of his anatomy had increased in girth, and she wasn't talking about his pecs anymore. His tongue swept into her mouth, the lingering hint of coffee vanishing as her taste buds switched to take him in. Clean, warm, and oh my God, the boy could kiss. Heat flushed from her core outward, her breasts grew hot and heavy, and damn if she remembered why she'd turned him away all these years. Strong fingers curled around her neck as he deepened their contact. She responded, her tongue brushing his, lips and teeth getting into the act. She grabbed his shoulders for support, digging into the firm muscles under her fingertips. He ate greedily at her mouth until her head spun, senses shifting to overload.

He snuck a hand around her torso, fingers spread wide as he slid under her shirt to caress the bare skin of her lower back. Warm palm in full contact with her body, he pulled her even tighter against his groin, and his rigid erection dug into her belly. Her breasts were crushed between them, nipples tight and aching. Max fastened onto her tongue and sucked it into his mouth, a flash of ecstasy shooting through her core and setting her on fire. How long had it been since she'd felt like this from simply kissing? She scraped her fingernails down his back and he dragged his lips from hers, groaning loudly. Air rushed back into her lungs, and she shoved her fingers into his back pockets and yanked him forward. The leg between hers nudged her knees farther apart before sliding closer to connect with her sex.

His assault on her senses continued as he worked his way along her jaw to press kisses and nips to the tender skin below her ear. The need inside escalated to the point she was ready to peel off her clothes and go for it right there. She was empty, and aching. Their combined breathing carried loud on the air, echoing in the hollow spaces of the unfinished room.

Max returned to her lips, thrusting his tongue into her mouth, mimicking the rocking motion of his hips, and she whimpered. It was too much and not nearly enough. He released his grip on her hair and cupped her ass instead, dragging her up his body until she rode the solid ridge of his erection. Tingling, flashes of heat, pleasure—all of it washed over her in waves and she clutched him tighter. Good Lord, she was going to climax like this, rubbing him like a cat.

He lifted her left leg higher and looped her knee over his elbow, forcing her back hard to the wall. Spread wide open, she was defenseless as he ground against her, the seam line of her jeans making contact with her clit through the thin layer of her thong and she panted hard. *So close.*

"Give it to me. Let me see…you…" He cut off and thrust, again and again. Muttered words drifted from his lips, his breath escaping in gasps. One more circular rotation with his hips, and she squeezed her eyes tight and tipped over the edge. Bliss bore down in rhythmic pulses, starting at the apex of her sex and spreading fingers through her core. She purred out her delight, accepting the orgasm and its continuing pleasure. He slowed his thrusts and recaptured her mouth, biting her lips, kissing her madly. Tasha leaned her head back to enjoy the aftershocks of her climax, taking delight in the attention he lavished on her.

They clung together, hands softening, lips slowing their feverish contact. Time slipped away. A buzzing fly drifted past their heads and pulled her from the haze of satisfaction settling heavy in her limbs.

He broke off their kiss, easing her down his body until her toes landed. He supported her, waiting for her to stop wavering on her feet. His chest moved in shallow breaths, obviously as affected by their actions as she. She glanced down and spotted his erection still bulging the front of his jeans. Remorse and doubt crept over her. Oh shit, what had she done?

He lifted her head and she stared into his eyes. The centers were dark, pupils dilated with lust. "You are so damn beautiful."

Max cupped her neck again, pulling her against his chest, and she'd never felt guiltier in her life. She listened to the pounding of his heart under her ear and let reality sneak back in. She had dry humped someone who she'd sworn to not get involved with sexually.

Who'd proposed to her thirty minutes ago and suggested he wanted nothing better than to get her pregnant.

Just as her mind protested vehemently, he cleared his

throat. His voice when he spoke was deeper than usual, husky with lust. "I needed that."

Madness. Sheer madness. Tasha pressed her palms against his chest in an attempt to separate their bodies. His arms were steel bands around her as he refused to let her go.

"You wouldn't be planning on running, would you?"

"I'm sorry, I shouldn't have done that. Oh God, I don't believe I let—"

"Let it happen? Don't lie. You wanted it as much as I did."

Well, shit. This had gone far enough. "Max..."

"Don't deny it. Don't regret it, I sure the hell don't."

Tasha shivered at the intense expression in his eyes. He wasn't going to let her make some flip remark and escape this time. She took a deep breath and let it out slowly. "I won't deny I enjoyed it, but we never should have started in the first place."

"We wanted to."

She wiggled and this time he released her. "Yeah, well, want and should aren't the same thing."

"You want to have a baby by yourself. Should you?"

Ice replaced the lingering heat in her veins. "That's not fair."

"My point exactly."

She looked away as Max adjusted his erection, stifling the impulse to offer to help him out. No matter how pissed off his final words made her, the desire to caress his naked skin under her fingers remained. He'd lit a fire inside and one orgasm wasn't enough to satisfy it. His hand touched her arm and tugged her to face him. A gentle touch under her chin brought their gazes back in line and he smiled. One part trouble, three parts sin.

"I wanted to prove that we are attracted to each other no

matter how much you've denied it. You're right—it's not enough to build a relationship on, but it's not a bad place to start."

All the fight faded from her. Between last night and this morning, between her rickety future plans and her dismal past agendas, she had nothing left inside right now.

"This was not how I imagined spending today," she admitted.

The cheeky grin she'd seen so often at Turner family events broke across his face. "I had planned on joining a gaming marathon, but this is far more exciting."

She wanted to roll her eyes. Him and his damn computers. "Sorry to have dragged you away from world domination."

"You know the Turners. There'll be another chance to play soon enough."

Max released his hold on her arm and retreated slowly. Cool air wafted between them and chilled her body. Something inside her heart ached as well. She wasn't supposed to want another person to keep her warm. She'd thought she was past that.

Tasha glanced outside at her future backyard. The clearing crew had managed to leave the big oak tree like she'd requested. One limb stretched horizontally, perfect for a tire swing down the road. It would be somewhere safe for a child to play while she watched out the window, or while she pushed them. Suddenly some of the murky details in the fantasy she'd been dreaming filled in. A child with dark hair, red highlights shining in the sun, and a mischievous smile. She caught her breath at the image of child like Max.

Her mind spun. Again, it was too much, too soon.

Max coughed. She turned to find he'd crossed the room. He stood beside the front door, holding it open. She moved slowly to join him and they made their way back to his car in silence.

Her brain was far too full of chaos to be able to speak rationally, and small talk would have been inappropriate.

He drove her home, the radio providing a blur of background noise to the thirty-minute ride between her new house in Frazer and her apartment in Thompson. The lack of sleep, the alcohol and the stress wrapped together, and she gave up any attempt at being polite. She stared out the window, nothing concrete in her mind except the dire need to crawl into bed and hibernate for days.

All the way from the parking lot to the door of her apartment he paced beside her, shortening his long stride to accommodate hers. When she paused in her doorway to speak he pressed a finger to her lips.

"You're tired and still hungover. Go to bed. Think about this when you're fresh."

Max placed the folder in her hand, and reached for her, and she held her breath. She didn't know what she'd do if he kissed her again. Something in her face must have warned him she was ready to crack and he froze. He cleared his throat and took a shaky breath before heading back to the elevator silently.

It was all she could do to make it to her bed and collapse, fully clothed. She tossed the file on her bedside table where it haunted her for the two minutes it took until she fell asleep.

Maxwell leaned back in his car seat and adjusted himself again. If he hadn't already earned sainthood status, he was well on the way. Fuck, kissing Tasha, touching her, bringing her to a climax, all of it had exceeded his expectations, and he'd had plenty. After years of sexual fantasies about the woman, this morning he'd been tempted to drag her to the floor and let her ride him.

He reached down and slid the seat farther back to wrangle

more room. Shit, he was dying. He'd been hard off and on since last night when he'd discovered what he'd pictured in his brain wasn't far off the mark. From the moment she'd shocked the hell out of him by pulling off her dress, he couldn't look away. Her breasts overflowed the skimpy cups of her bra, and he'd thought she'd skipped wearing panties altogether. It wasn't until she'd crawled into his arms that the tiny scrap of fabric pretending to be a thong became apparent. He'd had the warm, silky skin of her ass in his hands, her arms draped around his neck as she pressed his face between her breasts.

"Bloody hell. *Fuck!*" He swore a blue streak, flipped the radio to the dirtiest, raunchiest station he could find and cranked up the volume until the walls of the car pulsed around him.

Max thumped his cock hard, rubbing at the front of his jeans in an attempt to ease the pain. When she'd told him she was horny? That moment hadn't been the worst. Struggling to untangle himself and cover her up when what he wanted more than his next breath was to rip open his zipper and slam his cock into her as deep as possible—that had been far easier than the demons he had to fight when they reached her room.

She'd told him everything. In the space of fifteen minutes between unlocking her door and carrying her nearly naked body to her bed—and didn't that part make his nuts draw into tight little rocks at the memory—she never stopped talking. About what assholes her previous boyfriends had been. How they sucked in bed, and she got more pleasure from her fingers most of the time. How she yearned for a baby.

How incredible he smelled and did he want to make her feel good? She could go for a good, hard fuck.

Max smashed his fist into the steering wheel and ground his teeth together. Replaying in detail every second of last night wasn't helping. He'd gone home and jerked off, frantic to get relief, and it still hadn't worked. In the sleepless hours that followed, he'd put together his proposal.

He slammed his car into gear and headed home, careful to set the cruise control because in his current state of mind he was ripe to be pulled over for reckless driving. He'd wanted Tasha forever, and he swore they'd be good together, but would she be willing to admit it? She was almost as stubborn as he was, and she'd always, *always* pushed him away. Made him walk the line as a friend and nothing more.

Thank God they'd had the time over at the house. His mouth watered at the memory of her lips under his, her nails scraping down his back. He wanted to be naked, buried deep in her body and have her mark him then. He needed to listen to her moans as she approached climax.

Ahhh, *shit*. He needed a fucking cold shower.

Tasha would probably sleep like a log for most of the day. Then she'd stew and consider his offer from fifteen different angles before coming to a conclusion. He certainly intended on providing the guidance needed to push that decision in the right direction. Still, he couldn't do anything more today. Maxwell turned down the long driveway to his house with a heavy heart and a raging hard-on.

Right now, he hated waiting with a vengeance.

Chapter Four

His sister's car sat beside his house and Max swore. He didn't want to have to be polite and have a social visit with anyone, not even if he and his twin got along like gangbusters. He took another minute in an attempt to relax enough to walk the stairs without it being obvious he had the hard-on from hell.

He hadn't expected to see Maxine today. She waited for him on the front steps, a wistful expression on her face.

"Hey, Maxy, what's happening?"

She shrugged. "I'm supposed to go meet Mom and some of the aunties for a late lunch. Can I kill a little time with you?"

This was not what he'd been hoping for, with images of Tasha still filling his brain. Of course, whacking off in the shower didn't seem to help much. After getting a taste of reality, he was sick of using his imagination to be with Tasha. But how was he supposed to put his sister off when he'd always made time for her before?

"Course you can stay for a visit. Why didn't you wait inside?"

"It's too nice a day."

He forced a laugh, accepting her hug carefully, his hips twisted away so there wouldn't be the slightest chance she noticed anything. Together they stepped into the small cottage he owned that sat at the back of one of the estate homes. Maxine went to grab drinks while he wandered over to open the French doors to the deck. Years ago the cottage had been the gardener's living quarters. It was small, easy to keep tidy, and more than enough room for one person. It had been perfect when he'd returned from college and announced he wasn't going to live at home anymore. He still remembered how much his parents had balked at the idea—they'd had troubles accepting that he'd finished high school at an accelerated rate. Him being back from college at seventeen? That wasn't the norm for many kids to be done with school and wanting their independence, but Max had insisted. He had his own business; he had the money he needed. He was vocal enough and strong willed, and it wasn't often he didn't get his way.

Except, up to now, with Tasha.

Distraction. That's what he needed. Maybe the fact Maxine was here would give him something else to think about other than the taste of Natasha's lips under his, and the sounds she'd made when she climaxed.

Ah man...he needed to keep his thoughts on other things. Safe things, the kind he could talk about with his sister. He scrambled mentally for a second, then glanced over to make sure Maxine was listening. "I've got another client lined up for the final test drive of the new software. You interested in taking part in the presentation?"

She spun at the sink and beamed at him. "You serious?"

"Of course. I told you if you got your skills up on code I'd take you on as a partner."

She handed him a glass of ice tea, even as she shook her head. "No, we've been over this before. I can't be a partner. I've got nothing saved up to put into the business. I'm thrilled to work with you, but hire me, okay?"

They moved to sit outside in the old rattan chairs he'd found at a garage sale earlier in the summer. He'd pictured relaxing here with Tasha, the sun setting behind the trees. *Damn it, mind on the present.* "Yeah, yeah you keep saying that, but I think you've got tons to contribute. I loved what you did on the Turner Networking Team website. Very cool graphics on the TNT banner, by the way. How about this? I'll set you up as a partner based on a buy-in system. As you work projects you'll get so much in pay and so much in partnership credit. Would that make you feel better?"

Maxine nodded slowly. "Next year when we turn twenty-five, part of the Turner legacy funding will come through, and I can add in whatever the business needs as a full top-up."

He laughed. "What? You're actually planning on spending some of the *Max* money?"

"Goodness knows we deserve it. It would have been bad enough to have the same initials as all your cousins, but the same name?" She grimaced. "Although I've very grateful that Mom and Dad came up with decent Max names to meet the requirement of the legacy fund. Auntie Maxamule—I can't say her name without wanting to giggle."

"Maximilian is bad as well."

She wrinkled her nose. "Is it terrible to admit I don't like our cousin very much?"

Max leaned back in his chair and stretched his legs, letting the sun warm his face. Was Tasha asleep or thinking about his proposal? "He's a fake, that's why. You're too sweet to like someone who's a phony."

"I'm not sweet."

He guffawed. "Yes, you are."

"I'm not."

"Are too."

She narrowed her eyes and he made a face at her. "Oh, you're so grown-up."

They smiled at each other, their conversation having digressed back to twin-speak. Max looked his sister over as she sipped her tea. She *was* sweet, and innocent, and he was glad to be able to work with her. She had a soft heart, and he didn't mind watching over her, like any good brother would. In a family as big as the Turners, there was something happening all the time, and Maxine was usually right in the middle of it. He'd learned to withdraw a bit from the constant clannish demands, partly because he'd been working for himself since he'd discovered computers. Maxine never seemed to have learned to say no.

He opened his mouth to tell her about Tasha, then took a quick gulp of tea instead. Until he had something concrete to tell, he wasn't going to share. And until Tasha made a decision, there was nothing to convey.

It felt kind of strange, to keep a secret from Maxine. Not that he told her everything, but they were close. She chatted about something going on with a couple of their younger cousins over the past week, and he nodded and listened as best he could. All the while his thoughts drifted. Back to the soft touch of Tasha's skin under his fingers when he'd kissed her. To the taste of her lips. He could hardly wait to make love with her.

"What do you think?"

He jerked upright guiltily. "Sorry, Maxy, lost my train of thought for a minute."

She laughed. "Didn't get much sleep last night, hey? I heard you ended up driving Cousin Lila and her drinking buddies home. I thought I was the only one sweet enough to get suckered like that." She batted her eyes and he groaned.

"I didn't mind." No, he hadn't. Hadn't minded one bit. In terms of charitable acts, it ranked right up there as one of the most self-serving activities he'd ever taken part in.

He sat back and concentrated harder on Maxine. Tasha wouldn't be calling any time soon, and until tomorrow, his life was in limbo.

There was something hard poking her in the belly, and the most god-awful taste in her mouth. Tasha rolled over, tossed the shoe she'd found to the floor and winced as the sunshine pouring in the window stabbed her in the eyes. Okay, officially not the best way to spend a day. She levered herself vertical, fearful her head would spin, or her stomach.

It was her heart that did back flips when she spotted the file folder on the side table.

Maxwell Junior had proposed to her.

She wasn't sure which rose faster or higher—confusion or anger. He hadn't done anything on purpose to upset her, but damn it all, she'd had everything figured out. She was happy with her plan for artificial insemination. All the arguments he'd gone through she'd fought out with herself over the past months. There was no doubt in her mind that she'd be a fabulous mother, and any baby that did come along would be well loved and cared for. Still, she wasn't about to argue that two good parents couldn't provide even more, and she loved the thought of having extended family for her child.

But it wasn't possible. She'd tried the regular route of getting involved with a partner. She'd had no luck finding anyone she wanted to spend a year with, let alone long enough

41

to raise a child.

I like Max.

Her mind darted everywhere. It wasn't acceptable for him to come in and tear her world apart. Intoxicating kisses and magical orgasms aside, she had to do the right thing for the long run.

She poured herself into the shower and turned the heat up as hot as she could handle. The headache from the previous night's overindulgence had faded, exchanged for the dull ache of stress. She soaped her body, trying to ignore the tenderness between her legs from where he'd rubbed her to an orgasm. It was too easy to slip her fingers over the sensitive skin and daydream about what Max would do to her when she had her clothes off, his fingers touching her more intimately. Stoking and sliding over her skin...

Dammit, no. She would not fantasize thinking about Maxwell Turner. Tasha forced her hands away from her sex and did the fastest wash ever of her breasts, the tightness of her nipples taunting her.

Even when he was nowhere in the room, Max tormented her.

She dried herself, rough with the towel, then yanked on track pants and a T-shirt before stomping to the kitchen.

He had proposed to her.

Three glasses of water and an orange juice later, Natasha sat on her balcony in the sun, her eyes closed. Every deep breath she took in she mentally wrapped up one of her concerns and breathed it out. She needed to make a decision, but totally uptight and upset wasn't the way to go into anything.

She grabbed the notepad from the chair beside her and started another list.

He'd given her three reasons for them to be together. She listed them, neatly, in order. Made two columns to the right of each with room for pros and cons. There was no way to get to the bottom of this without some solid information. Knowing Max, if she phoned him right now he'd insist on far more than a simple yes or no. He'd want to know why.

She laughed in spite of the situation. Yeah, he'd said she knew him better than to simply say he was too young. He hadn't been too young mentally since fifth grade. The damn man was borderline genius. She couldn't accuse him of not having thought out all the angles.

Tasha blew out a long slow breath. Fine, then it was only right she do the same thing. She'd gone through this before when she'd made the decision to become a single mom. Once more wouldn't hurt.

The first item seemed the easiest, and safest, to deal with.

#1. Having a baby w/ Junior

Pros-

The words he'd shouted at her in the house made her smile. Colic and diapers. She had to admit she liked that he wasn't afraid to speak plainly to her.

She listed points under each category, everything she could think of. She winced as she wrote down *financial security.* She didn't like to admit that was one area she'd been the most nervous about regarding being a single mom. Even after getting to the point she had a solid home business, and enough money put away for the immediate future, what if something happened to her? She'd have insurance, but still.

#2. Having a baby with the extended Turner family around

Oh man. The lists grew fuller, on both the pro and con sides. Her family was a write-off. Her dad had disappeared a long time ago, and her mom was too busy with her own life on the other side of the country to give a damn. Tasha had settled on the west coast. She'd been friends with Lila for years, and Max was right, she'd attended more Turner-clan gatherings than she could count. The joys and downfalls of a large extended family were not a mystery to her. There were always willing hands to cuddle babies, wipe noses and read stories.

There were also tons of unasked-for opinions offered regarding personal issues. She swirled the glass of juice she'd refilled, watching the ice cubes spin in the bright liquid. Her privacy wasn't so important that the thought of the family scared her away, but there was something to be said about not having everyone in town know everything about your business.

#3. A long-term relationship, by choice, with Maxwell.

Tasha put down the pen. She wasn't willing to add to either the pro or con list right now. It was as if writing it in ink that would make it more real.

Was he someone she'd choose to be with?

Physically, there was nothing but dynamite between them. He'd proved that without a shadow of a doubt, her sex aching even now when she remembered his commanding touch. No, there would be hesitation when it came to writing that down as a positive. On the negative side—how long would it last? She'd done her best to stay in shape, but she was thirty-four. She planned on a having a baby. Would there be the same physical fireworks a year or two down the road? She couldn't count on it, not as a positive, and suddenly the current overwhelming attraction between them seemed less important in the big scheme of things.

Mentally—that was the one area she couldn't think of a single downfall. Max was smart, probably smarter than she was. Yet he wasn't mean about it like some people she knew who felt the need to rub in their superiority at every opportunity. He worked with others easily, and in that typical Turner style, he supported his family by finding ways to make their lives easier by using his brain.

Gack. Even thinking about it made him sound like some sort of incredible epitome of manhood who she'd be crazy to think about turning down.

The con side taunted her. It wasn't so much him, as his sex. A long-term relationship. What exactly did that mean to a twenty-four-year-old? She'd dated thirty-year-olds whose idea of forever was "until they spotted a better looking pair of legs". Coming home to find her partner in bed with another woman—not something she ever wanted to experience again. Being neglected, or having a new job in a new location chosen over her? Maybe she had the shittiest luck in who she'd gotten involved with over the years, but frankly her track record with guys was miserable.

Maybe it wasn't the guys' fault, maybe it was her. Hell, even in her own tiny family of origin she saw no indication she could be loved long term.

She knew she'd be there for a child, unconditionally, and forever. A devoted family of two wasn't a terrible thing to plan to achieve. Maybe it would be more physically challenging, and emotionally, she's have to go it alone. But she was certain having someone bounce in and out of her child's life was potentially much worse than never having daddy figure at all.

Tasha gave up. She put on her sneakers and headed out the door for a long, hard run. If nothing else, it would force the remaining alcohol out of her system. This coming week, no matter what she decided, she was going to move ahead with the baby making.

The question still remained whether or not Maxwell would be involved.

Chapter Five

Three days. Max flicked between computer screens, his edginess filtering out through his fingers. Three restless, incredibly long days—they each felt far longer than the standard twenty-four-hour period—and she still hadn't made up her mind. Max was caught somewhere between demanding an answer and waiting that one more day in case one wrong move would turn a potential yes into a no.

He'd seen her the day after he'd proposed. Stopped by her apartment first thing in the morning with a fresh herbal tea and a fruit smoothie. Tasha had been dressed but still sleepy eyed and soft looking, and he'd wanted to jump her right there.

She'd taken both his offerings with a nod, then ordered him to get his ass out and wait for her to call him. Her forceful response had made him smile—he'd put her out of kilter, had he? Of course, there were other ways to stay in contact. She'd said nothing about email.

But as the days passed, the urge to ignore her command and simply show up at her office increased, and he had to forcibly ignore it. The idea of sending flowers? He'd love to, but that kind of overture was romantic, and she wasn't looking for romance, she was looking for a forever friend. If he was going to sell her on this for long enough to be able to subtly influence her, he had to play by her rules right now. No matter how much it sucked.

He couldn't concentrate on his work and had taken to goofing off on his pet project instead, a new and more interactive website for Tasha's architecture business. Every time he popped onto her old site, his eyes wanted to bleed, with the bad color choices and static header. Not that he was trying to sweeten the pot or anything, but sending her an email to check the draft site would at least ensure he was put front and center in her mind.

He dragged another icon into place, adjusting the position when the Turner Alert web link went off. Someone, somewhere amongst his vast relative pool, had set up a game night. Thank God, that was just what he needed for distraction. He clicked the link and rejoiced. It was an open call from Lila, which meant he was invited, and the chances of seeing Tasha went from slim to nearly one hundred percent.

He saved his work then grabbed the phone. "Maxy—are you and your roommate going to need a ride to the game?"

His sister hesitated. "I don't think so. I mean, I don't."

Max shut down his computer and headed for his room to make a quick change of clothes. "Aren't you coming? I'll let you be on my team. Lila mentioned we're playing Taboo."

"I'm coming, but I...I already have a date for tonight."

Max stopped dead in his tracks. "A date? Really?"

She growled at him. "You're such a turkey. Yes, a date. I am old enough you know. It's not like I'm not allowed to spend time with the opposite sex."

Well, if he had anything to say about it, she would still be off limits. Yeah, pretty damn hypocritical considering he'd given Tasha heck for thinking he was too young a few days ago, but this was his *sister*. He beat down his protective urges. "Do I know the guy?"

"Junior…"

"What? You know you're going to get the third degree from everyone else, may as well practice now."

Her sigh carried over the phone, and he laughed to himself. He could picture her, slightly flustered and blushing red as she tried to come up with the best way to make this guy sound safe and yet interesting at the same time.

"He works at the college."

Teacher was good. "Does he have tenure?"

"Junior!"

He laughed. "Okay, no more teasing. Tell me straight, and I'll be a good big brother and shut up."

"Big brother, ha. By ten minutes."

"Take it up with Mom, not my fault."

Max hopped in his car, switched to his hands-free, and headed over to Lila's, listening as his sister rambled on about the new guy. He didn't sound too dangerous, although Maxine had dashed those first initial high points when she shared the guy wasn't a professor, but a clerk in shipping and receiving.

The sight of Tasha's car in the driveway of Lila's house made his heart do this crazy double thump. One way or another, she would be reminded that he was waiting for her response. He raced up the stairs and only managed at the last second to be polite enough to knock.

Eager beaver.

Laughter poured out the door as it opened, and he smiled, expecting to see his cousin. Instead he found himself looking into the brown eyes that had been haunting his dreams for the past days, weeks, heck—years, if he was honest.

"Junior." She clutched the door, her laughing face tightening into a frown, and he felt like a fool. Obviously his proposal had been so far out of line she had no idea how to turn him down. He stuttered for a second, disappointment and disillusionment sweeping through him.

"Tasha. Good to see you."

They stood there for a minute, staring at each other. Then he noticed her blush, and hope fluttered back to life.

She jerked upright. "Sorry, come on in." She opened the door and stepped back, and he slipped in past her, brushing as close as he could without making it noticeable to everyone in the room. He stood by her side and took a deep breath, her light perfume filling his head and making it spin.

"How have you been?" Tasha asked quietly as he looked around at the crowd gathering to play. She didn't run off to hide, which he took as a good sign. Damn, he'd take anything as a good sign right now.

Optimist, that was him. Either that or he was a glutton for punishment.

"Anxious. Fretful. Hopeful?"

"Don't..."

Max shrugged. "You asked. I was polite and didn't even mention the physical reactions I've been having." He gestured toward the kitchen. "Can I get you something?"

She sighed and walked beside him. "It's going to sound pathetic, but nothing sounds good to drink."

Right. Her self-imposed, chemical-free, all-natural, healthy-eating-and-drinking Operation Baby. After his stomach did a roll in sympathy for her, that spot inside him that made him want to go all protective and nurturing on her kicked into overdrive. "Come on, I'll give you a hand."

There were close to twenty people already wandering Lila's place—family, friends. The same people Max had spent many a night with over the years. He waved and exchanged greetings with them as he ushered Tasha forward. There was a strange expression on her face as he led her to an island chair and seated her.

He clued in—she was checking to see if anyone was watching them.

"They're used to seeing us together. You don't need to worry," he whispered in her ear before turning to the cupboard and helping himself to two glasses. He poured orange juice, topped it up with sparkling water, then returned to her side.

"I wasn't worried." She took the glass he offered, while yet another sigh escaped.

He raised a brow and sipped his juice.

"Okay, stop that. I haven't made a decision, so yes, I am worried. I don't want anyone getting the wrong idea." She spoke quietly. Her fingers fumbled with her glass as she greeted another family member moving past them to dig into the fridge.

Max patted her knee lightly, a teasing touch. "Relax." Her gaze kept darting everywhere as people wandered in and out of the kitchen, grabbing what they needed. "Seriously, no one thinks anything of seeing us together—watch this."

He turned to the couple leaning on the other side of the island. "Dave, Carole. You guys got your team together for the night?"

Dave grinned. "You offering to join us?"

Max winked. "Why not—my sis isn't here yet, I might as well give you guys a hand kicking Lila's butt." He rose and knocked knuckles with Dave, ignoring Tasha where she now sat alone. About five seconds is all he figured he should have to wait.

Tasha fought to keep from frowning. He'd left her? Joined another team? Her sense of disappointment was as instant as it was shocking. She sat up straighter, trying to figure out what to say.

Carole turned from where she'd just given Max a big hug. "Oh, hey, Natasha. You have a team yet? You want to join us as well?" Carole stopped dead as if realizing something. "If that's okay with you, Max. Did you have another partner already?"

Tasha gazed across the room at Max's grinning face. The bastard raised a brow and grinned. "No partner. Tasha can join us. I don't mind."

Dave nodded once. "I'll go nab us a spot, otherwise we'll be crowded on that damn broken couch again. The springs are enough to kill me." Carole grabbed their glasses and the two of them bombed out of the room.

Max leaned on the island across from her, his biceps pressing the fabric of his T-shirt. She dragged her gaze higher to meet his eyes. Laughter reflected back.

She glanced around the room, making sure there was no one near enough to overhear them. The kitchen had emptied, everyone else already congregating in the other room. "You're such a wise-ass, aren't you? Your point is everyone is used to seeing us together, without thinking of us as being together."

He stared at her lips and she fought the urge to lick them. "Right now, that's the truth. I'd love to have them see us a couple."

Tasha sat up rigid in her seat. "Junior."

"I'm being honest. The fact is moving this relationship forward is right, Tasha. It's right for you, and me, and it's perfect for the baby you're going to—"

"Stop." My God, he was driving her insane. There was a part deep inside that wanted to simply throw herself at him and

51

accept his offer. The other part? Wanted to run far, far away. She obviously was having a split-personality issue. "Not tonight. I'm here to relax. Just—let's go play and not discuss this right now."

His expression revealed more than he probably wanted it to. She wished she had an answer for him, but sitting on the fence still felt pretty damn comfortable. He guided her into the living room, his hand warm on her arm. They sat next to each other on the love seat Dave had claimed, crowded together, his thigh tight against hers. Every brush, every twitch, brought a part of her body into contact with his, and every bit of contact caused a reaction. Her breath sped up, her heart pounded. As the game progressed, her ability to concentrate rapidly diminished.

The laughter filling the room echoed in her ears, hollow. She was too distracted by the warmth of his touch, the casual way he leaned against her as he laughed at Carole's attempts to play. As another team groaned over being caught cheating. All her senses were on high alert, and every one of them wanted him to be deliberately using his considerable talent on her.

But it was only physical attraction. Damn the way her nerves tingled, it wasn't enough to make forever happen.

Maxwell stiffened beside her when over an hour after the game had begun, his sister arrived with her date. Tasha did a double take, as did all the other girls in the room.

"Oh my, where did Maxy find him?" someone whispered.

The guy was gorgeous, with longish blond hair, face of an angel. Maxwell's twin introduced him as Jamie, and as they joined in one of the groups, Maxwell's head swiveled to watch them closely.

Even with Maxwell distracted, it wasn't enough to interrupt Tasha's obsession with his casual touch. Her mind raced, to the point that her attention span disappeared. She could barely play during their turn. She had trouble remembering to say polite goodbyes as the game broke up. People flitted around the room and began the trek out the door. All the while, the distracting warmth of his body hovered in close proximity.

It was like her brain had turned into some kind of Maxwell-tracking-device, to the exclusion of everything else. A trace of anger flared.

He smoothed a hand down her arm and she jerked away, deliberately stepping back a few paces to put some space between them. Surprise registered on his face.

"Can I walk you out?" Maxwell asked. Casual, friendly, just like always. No one around them even blinked, but Tasha held on to that flicker of heat. She was pissed at him, and at herself.

She couldn't make this kind of decision based on the physical rush he gave her. It wasn't enough—there were too many single moms to prove that fireworks in the sex department didn't mean the guy would stick around.

"No thanks, I'm good." She deliberately turned her back on him and grabbed Lila's attention, hauling her friend off and asking some impulsive questions.

Lila eyed her strangely as the rest of the gamers poured out the door.

"Okay, girlfriend. Enough already."

Tasha found herself dragged back into the kitchen once more and pressed onto one of the bar stools. Defensive instinct kicked in, and she started cleaning, stacking all the glasses within an arm's reach.

"What's wrong with you?" Lila asked. "I've seen eight-year-olds more with it the night before Christmas. You having troubles with a project or something? Because you're certainly not here right now."

Tasha shrugged, carrying a handful of glasses to the sink, wiping down the countertop. She grabbed at the excuse Lila offered. "Couple of projects on the go got me distracted. Sorry, I didn't think it was that noticeable."

Lila stared suspiciously. "Fine. Whatever it is you'll tell me when you're ready, I suppose. Now, can I get your opinion on a truly curious subject?"

Had Lila noticed something strange about all the attention she'd received tonight from Maxwell? "What?"

"Where the hell did my cousin Maxy find that guy, and do you think there are more lying around? I mean, I'm not in the market for anyone long term, but for a one-night stand? Holy moley, he was fine."

A laugh escaped. "He reminded me of a swashbuckling pirate."

They chatted for a short time before Tasha could make her escape. The evening hadn't turned out to be the relaxing getaway she'd hoped for. The long drive back to her apartment was lonely and silent. The laughter of the evening dissipated like a mess of bubbles on the air.

When she checked her inbox one last time before heading to bed, the reminder of the next doctor's appointment brought a fresh rush of tension to her shoulders, and crying herself to sleep seemed appropriate.

Chapter Six

Tasha placed the enormous tray of cookies and chocolates she'd brought as her contribution on the table, dodged around a group of children playing on the floor and headed out to the porch where she'd seen the older cousins gathering. She'd had enough of hiding out in her house, trying to make a decision. Joining Gramma Turner's birthday party seemed a safe alternative. Meeting Maxwell tonight was inevitable, but she figured there were enough people around she wouldn't have to be alone with him.

He'd taken to emailing her. She refused to see him—she didn't need the physical attraction between them distracting her as she reasoned this out. And yeah, that attraction was there, she wouldn't deny it. But emails? Relatively safe, since she set the pace and could respond when she wanted.

She'd opened the first few out of curiosity to see what tack he would take. After the initial I'm-being-stalked sensation wore off, she'd decided to make it a game to see how he reacted to her responses. It had been amusing—a couple words or a smilie, and he'd do the same, then leave her alone for a while. A full sentence response or more on her part was matched. Light-hearted, random information she was sure he'd purposefully chosen to make her smile, and to cause her to wonder what he was up to.

He didn't push for an answer, but he was always there, right in her face. One of the messages had shown up on her Blackberry when she was gown-draped and waiting in the doctor's office for another intrusive test before the official AI steps could begin.

That had been a hell she had no words to describe.

The invitation to attend the party had been too good to turn down. Gramma was a legend in the Turner family, now a widow for fifteen years, but still a powerhouse in keeping the clan together.

"Tasha!" Lila greeted her with a hug and drew her into the mix of thirty-something's mingling with the few older Turner clan who hadn't been lured off into games or dinner prep yet. Tasha looked around quickly, but saw no sign of Maxwell. Someone passed her an ice tea, someone found her a chair, and she was dragged into their discussion. Happiness rolled over her as she set aside her worries for a while and just visited.

Somehow the group around her changed, and Tasha found herself neck deep in conversation with Lila's grandmother, talking about everything from the hedges along the driveway to the summer's wasp problem. The crowd dissipated as people headed into the house and out onto the lawn of the massive heritage home Gramma Turner occupied. Tasha smiled at the old woman's expression—her pleased look as she surveyed her kingdom. It was a beautiful house, a part of the family legacy for years. The designer part of Tasha eyeballed the exacting bits that did work, and fiddled with the parts that didn't. She loved the solid wood arch brackets on the porch supports and the gable wings on the peak under the eaves and tried to figure out how she could slip some of those designs into her own house.

"It's good to talk with you tonight." Gramma Turner eyed her with approval. "Although, you do seem soul tired."

The children racing across the lawn caught her eye, and Tasha deliberately turned her chair to face the house and Gramma Turner more directly. "Life gets busy at times. I need a holiday, that's all."

"Oh, life does get busy, you're right about that." The older woman shook her head. "I've wondered what it would have been like to be rich, living in a fancy house like this one back in the days when the servant rooms were full and the master and mistress were waited on hand and foot."

Tasha wrinkled her nose. "I don't think I'd have liked that very much."

"You and me both. Although it's nice to be able to sleep in now that I'm not looking after babies and young ones. Maybe it's part of being with this whole crazy family, but I kind of think I'd be lost without the chaos that's always around."

It was chaos. Happy, controlled chaos with a hearty dollop of joy stirred in. Tasha risked taking a peek at the yard, the youngsters gathered together all lying on their bellies examining something in the grass as their older cousins reined them in.

Gramma Turner leaned back in her chair. "Well, that's enough of me flipping my tongue—see why they shouldn't make me sit and not let me stay busy in the kitchen? I'd talk your ear off if I had half a chance."

"It's your birthday. I think they wanted to make the meal a surprise. And if you cook it, it won't be," Tasha teased.

The older woman squeezed Tasha's hand again. "Just so you know—everyone here has a place in my heart, and that includes you, dear."

"You're amazing." Tasha gave her a sincere smile, a bit of a lump in her throat. This was the grandmother she'd never had.

"Tosh. I'm a very ordinary woman who's lived life as best I can. I love my family and work with my hands, that's all."

A bell rang in the distance, announcing the next portion of the evening was about to begin and Gramma Turner rose to her feet and took Tasha's arm. "Now. They managed to make me stay away while they served up dinner, but that's as long as I'm willing to sit on my behind like a lady of leisure. After supper, I'll be doing my amazing work in the kitchen washing dishes, and I'll be happy as a clam. It doesn't take much to please an old woman like me, you know. Give me a little food and drink, a warm roof over my head, and let me have my family around me and that's all I need."

Tasha led her into the house where Gramma was taken by the hand and brought by one of her grandsons to the place of honor at the head of the table. Tasha dodged back as bodies swirled around her, the voices on the air loud and happy, ringing with pleasure and the occasional childish complaint of who had to sit next to whom.

Tasha turned and found herself looking into a pair of big brown eyes. Maxwell smiled warmly as he led her to a chair, but he didn't say a word other than to make sure she was comfortable before he left. Tasha twisted her head to watch him as he took his place at the children's table with three of the other guys.

Lila passed the water pitcher down and nudged her, bringing her focus back to what was happening in front of her. "Got any plans for the rest of the weekend? You want to get together?"

"I've got a few projects I need to finish up, and I have to stop by the house to check the builder's progress, but other than that, I'm free." Tasha hid a smile as one of the children tried to escape from the children's table. Junior caught him easily, pulled the boy into his lap and enticed him with a few tidbits of food, all the while maintaining his conversation with the other older men guarding the children.

Lila followed her gaze and laughed. "Best. Tradition. Ever."

"Having the older Turner boys watch the little ones during dinner?"

"Hell, yeah. It almost makes up for having to have the Max in our names."

Tasha smiled. "I have to say I've always loved seeing that. None of the guys seem to mind, either. In fact if anything it's like they compete for the right to sit at the kids table."

"That's because sometimes it's funny as shit."

Tasha wasn't just watching the humor in the situation, although it did seem there was more food-wearing than food-consuming happening at moments. The half-dozen Turner males in charge, aged from late teens to late twenties, had their hands full, but there were no screaming children complaining about the situation. There was laughter, and joking, and a heavy dose of camaraderie.

"I wonder if it's like a test of knighthood—survive your family children's table duty and you are now one of us. I've never noticed the girls having to do it."

"They get enough watching time during the rest of the evening when the rugrats are free and on the run." Lila snickered and pointed to the side. "I think they should include dates in the tradition. Maxy's new beau looks horrified. I wonder how he'd handle the mashed-potatoes-in-the-hair trick?"

Tasha managed to keep eating, and chatting, but through it all that list of pros and cons she'd labored so hard over kept coming back to her again and again. And with every fleeting glance to see what Junior was up to, another one of her doubts slipped away. Across the room, laughter burst from a dozen throats at a time. Steady low conversations created a backdrop for the most erratic outbreaks of mirth. Gramma Turner's aged tones carried through the room, her wisdom and patience a kind of binder twine—a bright ribbon of love weaving through them all, and Natasha had to wipe away tears.

There was no way she could deny this to her child. No way that she could be all and everything to them. Having been offered a chance to join into such openly offered love, she would be a fool to turn it down.

She peeked again in Junior's direction, and this time caught him looking at her. There was hunger in his eyes, and a determination that switched immediately to a slightly cocky smile. He leaned back, acknowledging her, his hands holding firmly to the young child in his arms. Even as she watched, the little one wiggled around to plant a big kiss on his cheek, and suddenly Max's attention turned, the delight on his face clear. It wasn't a show for her sake, something to impress her with his goodwill. He was actually enjoying his time with the toddlers, and her final resistance stripped away.

He was a good man, and he had offered to make her dream come true. The fact he wanted to get married? It wasn't her first choice, but considering everything, surely that was the one thing she could give in return.

Somehow, she had to find the courage to tell him she would be willing to go ahead, at least with part of his proposal.

"Can I talk to you?"

Finally. Maxwell turned to discover the object of his past hour's search standing only a foot away. "I thought you'd joined the younger gang in playing hide and seek. You've been very elusive tonight."

Tasha nodded slowly. There was something different in her body language, something restrained. The dark marks under her eyes proved she'd been struggling to sleep well, and it drove him mad. He didn't want her to hurt like this. "I was staying away from you. That big window seat upstairs was a great place to sit and think for a while. I've come to a decision. You want to meet me somewhere?"

The knot in his belly tightened. "Serious, huh?"

"Very."

"Damn, maybe we should do this in public, so I don't lose anything vital if it gets messy." Somehow, he needed to keep the conversation light-hearted. It wasn't so much that he wanted to stop her from seeing how much this meant to him. It was one thing to fight for what he wanted, another to guilt the woman into a decision she didn't want to make.

She rewarded his effort by smirking.

"I'm not kicking you in the nuts, Maxwell. But we do need to talk." Tasha took a big breath. Looked around cautiously. "Maybe we could meet back at your house."

Their gazes connected and he peeled away the layers of innuendo in a flash. Freaking A, could it be? "Holy shit. Really?"

She held up a hand. "Just to talk. We need to make a few decisions and I don't want to... I mean, I don't think we should... We need to talk."

His brain and body fought a battle for which could react the fastest. She was accepting his proposal. He was going to be with the woman he'd longed for his entire life. They were going to have sex and start a lifetime together. And have sex.

Rational conversations were not high on his list right now.

The party was breaking up, there was no reason for them to stick around any longer. "I need to say good night to my Gramma, then I'll meet you at my place." He pulled his keys from his pocket and separated off the one for the house. "Here.

If you beat me home, make yourself comfortable."

Tasha bit her lip, cheeks flashing to red, and he swore.

"Shit, no, I didn't mean that in the sexually loaded way it came out. I mean, you want to talk, we'll talk. I get that. I promise I won't...push you for anything else tonight."

Although how he'd keep that promise he had no idea.

Someone called Tasha's name and she raised a hand in acknowledgement. She stepped back a pace and let her gaze drop over him, the heat that rose in her eyes doing nothing to inhibit his anticipation. She turned to leave, her ass swinging from side to side as she walked. He couldn't tear his gaze away, images of stripping her clothes off piece-by-piece filling his mind, only this time he'd indulge his every whim as far as it came to her body.

He tried to hurry, but while he cut his farewells short, there still were a lot of them to make. By the time he'd given his Gramma a kiss, hugged his parents, and extracted himself from the smallest of the cousins who clung to his ankles like burrs, his brain was feverishly repeating the images of Tasha, naked. Only this time she was in his bed, waiting for him.

His sister Maxine stepped in front of him.

"You haven't had a chance to meet Jamie yet." She gestured to the side. "I wondered if you wanted to join us for a coffee or something for a few minutes."

The only thing that could pull his feet to a complete stop would be this guy. Jamie had hung around Maxine all evening, never getting involved or joining any of the games. And since Maxine had been in the thick of helping everyone as usual, that meant her date had been holding up a wall and being a lump. In the eyes of the Turner clan, his actions screamed *loser*.

Fuck. "I can't go out, I've got a...meeting in a bit. But I do want to get together with you guys." Maxwell eyed Jamie with suspicion. "Tomorrow afternoon might work." Unless he was busy in bed with Tasha. His groin reacted to the mere thought, and he retreated to grab his coat.

"You've got a meeting tonight? After the birthday party?" Maxy sounded totally confused.

Shit—he wasn't about to lie to her. Not now. He whispered in her ear. "I've got a date. I don't want to visit with you and Mr. GQ right now, okay?"

She frowned. "You have a date? You didn't tell me you'd given up mooning over Natasha Bellingham."

Crap. Maxwell looked around the room to see if anyone had overheard. "I should have guessed you'd have spotted that."

"Like, duh, of course I did. You've been interested in her forever."

This wasn't good, not before he actually spoke with Tasha to confirm exactly what she had in mind. "Look, I can't talk right now, but I do want to visit with you. Soon. Let me call you tomorrow, and we'll set up a time, okay? And don't go telling anyone about my date yet. I'll explain the next time I talk to you."

Maxine shrugged. "Fine. I'll chat with you tomorrow." She kissed his cheek lightly, then held out a hand to Jamie. The man took her fingers in his and, without a word, waggled his brows at Junior and led her away.

Every instinct in him called for Maxwell to follow them and demand that coffee, right here, right now. And to demand that Jamie get his smirking grin and sticky fingers off his sister...but he had to let go sometime.

He stomped off across the lawn to where he'd tucked his car and pulled out cautiously, avoiding the rest of the family making their escape. It wasn't just that he had Tasha waiting for him back at the house, it was time he let his sister make her own decisions. She wasn't an idiot. Innocent maybe, but she was smart enough to be able to stop things that she didn't want to happen. If Jamie got out of line, she'd been shown by a lot of the family how to physically defend herself.

It took most of the trip home to placate his guilt, but he managed, and by the time he parked next to Tasha's fiery red Fiat, the only thing on his mind was her.

Chapter Seven

She'd opened the door carefully, walking into his house with trepidation. She felt like an interloper, someone coming in under false pretenses. She'd been in the tidy cottage before, any number of times, but never alone. Certainly never with the intent of being alone...with him.

She had to pull off her jacket, the heat that flushed her body enough to make the place rather warm. Junior had left music playing, and a rock beat pulsed through the house as she clicked on lights. For a guy's domain, it wasn't bad. She unashamedly snooped through the fridge, and around the living room. He didn't even have dirty dishes in the sink. The toilet seat was up in the bathroom, but other than that, and the unmade bed, his place was probably cleaner than hers.

On the desk in the corner, she spotted a pad of paper similar to the type she used for jotting notes while designing a house. She grabbed it and a pen before curling up in the loveseat. There was no doubt in her mind anymore that she wanted to accept his offer, but she needed to make sure this was a totally rational decision.

That night at the party she'd been hit with a powerful picture of the unconditional love and support the Turners offered. The large clan was sometimes overpowering, but always entertaining, and the images of the many things she'd missed over the years flooded her heart and mind. She had no extended family anywhere in this part of the country, but she'd deliberately made her home here. Her mom was remarried, and didn't seem to want her around. Natasha wrote a word at the top of the page, underlining it carefully. She desperately wanted to have a baby, but she needed to consider the best thing in the long run for her child.

Having a larger group of family around, including a full-time father—there was no way she could deny her child that part of an upbringing. Since she seemed to have no luck in having people love her for the long run, the temptation to make her child's world as perfect as possible was too much to resist. She wrote quickly, all thoughts of the physical attraction between her and Maxwell pushed aside. This was too important to lose focus right now. It wasn't about having someone permanently in *her* life, it was about providing for her baby.

She was concentrating so hard on her writing that when the door opened she jerked in surprise, her head shooting up to find Maxwell rapidly approaching, his coat and keys tossed haphazardly on the table. She scrambled to grab the notepad from where it had fallen on the floor, catching the edge of the paper the same moment he did.

They lifted it together and his eyes distracted her. The dark centers dilated wider as he stared at her, crouched low beside the chair.

"Hey."

She swallowed hard. "Hey. You weren't as long as I thought you'd be."

He dropped the notepad to the side, his eyes hungrily tracing her face as he grabbed her hand. "I broke the speed limit. By a lot."

She chewed on her lower lip. All the confidence she'd had

back at the house when she'd told him she wanted to speak with him seemed to have escaped, fleeing into the night. "That's not very responsible of you."

"I'll be responsible from here on, but if I didn't hear you actually say it, I was going to go insane. Are you accepting my offer? Will you marry me?"

She pulled her hand from his and nodded slowly, reaching for the notepad. "Yes, but with a few conditions."

Maxwell stiffened slightly. "What kind of conditions?"

"If you're worried about not getting sex, that's not it," she joked, desperately trying to lighten the mood. She was one step away from freaking out as it was.

He rose to his feet in one motion. "This isn't a gag, Tasha. Yes, I want to have sex with you, but I've damn well offered my life to you and this baby. I'm giving you everything I can think of that's important to me, so I'd appreciate a little mutual respect. This isn't about simply wanting to get into your pants."

Shit. She popped up after him, shaking her head rapidly. "Damn it, that's not what I meant."

"But that's what you said. That's all I've got to go on." He dragged a hand through his hair before pulling to a stop. "I'm sorry, I'm more on edge than I thought. You don't deserve to be shouted at."

She held the notepad to him. "If you'd give me a second I can explain. The only conditions involve us as a couple."

He took the paper and rotated it to read. "A prenatal agreement?"

"It was the best I could come up with on short notice." *Fuck.* Her voice quivered. She wanted to be in charge and in control, and instead the whole situation was making her weepy and morose. She cleared her throat and squared her shoulders.

Max sighed, then held out his hand to her. He was far too astute. She slowly accepted his offered hand, let him pull her into his arms and hold her close for a minute. His heart beat strong against her chest, the brush of his lips against her hair a soft flickering breeze. He squeezed her tight before letting her go, tugging her instead to his side as he sat them on the couch.

"Okay, let's look this over. I hope you don't mind if I play with it a bit?"

"Of course not. I want this to work for you as well—it's got to be fair and right for us both. I think we should probably get some papers drawn up formally." She curled her legs up beside her, leaning against his side before she'd realized it. The warmth of his body helped keep her jitters away, and she gave in to the temptation to stay there. "I guess the main things are making sure that we've got this figured out financially, and with the family. If for some reason I can't get pregnant, I don't want you to feel like you're trapped into staying with me."

Max hummed as he added notes to the paper. "If you can't get pregnant, it could be my fault. We'll deal with it if that happens. Worst-case scenario—have you thought about adopting?"

She shrugged. "I have, but that wouldn't be anything for you to be concerned about."

He twisted to face her. "You're simply not getting it, are you? There is no difference between a child that pops from your body, and one you adopt. They both need family around. I'm in, for the long haul. If we make a baby, great. If not, we adopt and the Turner clan will grow that way."

The lump in her throat was enormous. She was smart enough to bite back the words asking if he was sure. The expression on his face said he was.

"Tasha? Did you understand what I said?"

She nodded, and he crossed off one of her paragraphs on the prenatal agreement. The only out-clause she'd given him.

He pointed down the page. "You don't have to worry about the money part. I've got a fair bit saved up, and this house can be sold. We can set up some accounts together and some apart—however you feel the most comfortable, but I can tell you right now I make enough to support us both."

She pressed her hand over his mouth. "Junior, I'm not worried about the money. I trust you. My God, you're a genius. If anything, you should have the papers drawn up so my business doesn't suck yours under. That's not what I want to tell you."

He leaned back, twisting to the side against the arm of the couch so he could face her.

"I'm not in love with you."

Max shrugged. "I didn't say you were."

Tasha shook her head. "I'm not planning on falling in love with you. I mean, I like you, and I admire you. But I want us to be there for this baby, and that's the bottom line. This isn't about roses and poetry. It's a commitment to the family, and friendship. Nothing more."

He didn't even blink. "Okay."

That easy? Tasha looked for even a glimmer of amusement or ridicule on his face. It wasn't there. In fact, his expression was basically unreadable. "Okay?"

Max reached and cupped her chin. His thumb brushed against her cheek softly. "I said before that we were going into this by choice. I choose to be with you. You've made my motor run over the years, but I've also admired your work and your energy and your enthusiasm for life. That's why I want to be with you. I don't need any mystical emotional rush to convince me to entangle my future with yours."

69

Tasha stared at him. With one word, her life would change, the entire direction she'd set in motion blown apart. Was it really the right thing to do?

"Friends?" she asked.

"As always. And lovers. Hopefully soon, parents." She nodded. Maxwell's gaze shifted away from her eyes and dropped to where she'd nervously bit her lower lip. "I think this calls for a celebration, don't you?"

He leaned forward and caught her mouth against his.

Max had been longing for this moment. He understood why she felt they had to talk through the situation, but as far as he was concerned, all the rest of the details were minor irritations they could deal with anytime. As he kissed her, her mouth opening under his caress, he was struck by how perfect it was, to be here in his house for their first time together. The place he'd established as part of his independence. Then she wrapped her arms around his neck, tangled her fingers in his hair and all thought fled, replaced instead by a fever in his veins that threatened to ignite his whole body. Her lips were soft, but her kisses were as demanding as his own. There was no pretending that she didn't want him, no pretense this was some clinical motion they were going to complete.

Max twisted her on the couch, adjusting so she lay half under him, her body resting on the firm surface, his body resting on hers and his mind boggled. Warm thighs, soft breasts, those lips that continued to drive him mad with slow, wet kisses. The urge to speed up, to eat her hungrily was dismissed in a flash—this was too important to skip the preliminaries. They may have been friends forever, but the lovers bit was shiny and new. Even as eager as he was, he had enough control for that. Maybe.

The kissing went on and on, her mouth beckoning him back. He longed to unwrap her, take this to the logical conclusion, but the distraction of her willing lips was irresistible nectar. She touched and teased with her tongue, a temptress with enough skill to make his knees weak.

Tasha unbuttoned his shirt, kissed along his jaw then bit his neck. He rolled them slightly to one side to let him get at her clothing. He smoothed a hand along the curve of her breast, down her waist, over the swell of her hip until he could cup her ass and pull her close. His cock ached, and grinding against her gave only a momentary relief. He needed to strip her bare, haul her to the edge of the couch and drive in as deep as he could.

Her tongue was doing wicked things to his neck but he wanted more than her lips on his skin. He dug his fingers into her hair and tilted her head back until her mouth was in reach and he could kiss her again. He reveled in her taste, but mostly he enjoyed the eager way she returned his touch.

Their hands were everywhere—opening shirts, tugging fabric from shoulders. They twisted together, staying in contact, feverishly connecting skin on skin as Max sat up and Tasha crawled over him, straddling his lap to return to kissing once more. It was like they were starving, and somehow sharing air would help them survive. He'd lost his shirt, she'd lost hers. Her bra still separated them and he wrapped her close, massaging her back, the warmth of her skin under his palms making him crazy.

It took three attempts to get the damn bra fastener open, and by that time Tasha was laughing, her soft giggles against his lips making him smile.

"Such smooth moves..."

"Distraction—my coordination can't take it. Holy shit, you're gorgeous." Max pulled the straps from her shoulders and stared as her breasts were revealed. He looked up into her eyes, heat reflecting back at him. "Seriously gorgeous."

He brushed a tender kiss on her lips before leaning back to admire her again. His mouth had gone totally dry.

The full swells of her breasts moved uneasily with her erratic breathing. He cupped one, lifting its heavy weight into his hand as he bent forward to lick the tip. A small sound escaped her. Tasha held his head and pulled him closer, and he gave in to what he'd longed for ever since her birthday. He latched onto the nipple and sucked it into his mouth, playing his tongue over the tip. The peak tightened and he nibbled lightly on the rigid point, pulling off with a slight suction to start all over on the other side.

He was in heaven. Warm skin, lovely heavy tits to enjoy, Tasha making the most fabulous noises in response to his actions. She rocked over him, her crotch heavy against his groin. The heat of her body bled down to entice him with the need to be surrounded by her, squeezing him close. Suddenly the couch was an absolutely rotten place to be, and he seized her under the hips and shuffled upright. Tasha grabbed his neck with a squeal.

"Max!"

"Bedroom. I want to be able to see you and touch you and not worry about falling off the edge of the damn couch."

She laughed. "I can walk."

"When I'm done with you, you won't be able to."

Her lips latched onto his neck again and a shiver raced down his spine. Damn, she'd found his sweet spot without even trying.

He stumbled to the bedroom, pushing the door aside with his shoulder. He dropped her to the bed surface and yanked the messy sheets to the floor. There were far too many clothes between the two of them still. He stopped for a moment to kiss her senseless, his body covering hers.

When he pulled away she groaned out her pleasure. "I didn't think we were going to—holy shit."

He'd stripped off her pants and panties in one motion, opened her legs and dropped between them. She was wet, the curls covering her mound moist where her cream had escaped. He took great pleasure in drawing a finger along her slit, separating her and opening her to his admiration. Her clit peeked out from the folds of skin at the apex of her opening, and he leaned forward to kiss her intimately.

Her hips bucked beneath his mouth, and he laughed. "You need me to restrain you or something?"

She lifted up on her elbows to see him better, her breasts distracting him for a second before he dragged his gaze back up to her eyes. "I'm not used to guys going down on me before I've given them head and promised them the moon."

A jealous pang raced through him. "Assholes. I'm the only one who gets to touch you, ever again. And I want to touch you everywhere."

The naked hunger in her eyes combined with the naked skin before him was enough of an answer, but she said it anyway. "Feel free."

He licked her slowly, scooping the taste of her onto his tongue before taking a swirl around her clit. Teasing the sensitive point, loving the moans that rose as he learned what pleased her.

The phone rang, and he ignored it. That's what answering machines were for. He delved in deeper, opening her with one hand, pulling her curls aside to let him continue to tease with his tongue. Long slow strokes, one after another, until her hips shook and he had to pin her down with his free arm.

Goddamn, he wanted to strip off his jeans and release his erection. Let her wrap her lips around him and see his shaft entering her mouth, her sex. Her ass—he wanted every inch of her to be marked by his touch. More than once. Maybe more than once tonight even.

He slipped a finger into her, relishing the wet heat surrounding him.

"Oh, yeah."

He chuckled. "*Oh yeah* to which? This?" He added another finger, pumping them lazily in and out, circling her labia, then pressing in deep. He stroked the front of her passage, hoping to find the places that would drive her mad as he listened carefully for her response.

"This?" He covered her with his mouth again, sucking her clit. He pulled the nub between his teeth and nibbled lightly. "You tell me what you like and I'm game to try."

"*Jesus.* How can you talk while you're fooling around?"

He lapped harder for a moment and her body tightened. He eased off as he felt the first flutters of her core around his fingers. "I like talking when I'm fooling around. I like to tell you the dirty things I want to do to you. You make me hot."

Tasha growled at him. "Bastard. I was so close."

"I know, but you'll get there again. And again. And again." He attacked, suckling her clit, finger-fucking her hard, and this time he didn't stop. He carried on until she shook under his touch, crying out her pleasure. Her hips rocked beneath him but he refused to slow down, driving her back up again with his mouth and fingers. This time he drew some of the moisture from her core down between her legs to the star hidden between her cheeks.

He pressed his tongue deep into her sex while he played with her ass and her cries of delight continued. She dragged her fingers through his hair, her knees pulled high and wide to allow him access. He was in heaven, and they'd only begun.

His phone rang again.

A second later, so did his cell phone. His sister's ring tone shrilled out.

He ignored them both, slipping his finger past the tight muscle of her ass as he slid his thumb into her sex. She squeezed around him and he pinched lightly, to make her squirm.

"Max."

He licked his way up her body as he returned to her breasts. Blood rushed through him, the need to touch her everywhere and the need to back off for long enough to strip down warring together.

The phones rang again. Tasha cupped his face, forcing him to look up at her. "Max, you've got to answer that."

"Screw the phones."

She laughed. "I can't screw anything with them ringing."

He reluctantly pulled away, staring at her naked body with longing. "Somebody better be dead."

"Max!" Tasha slapped his chest and crawled backward on the bed.

It was painful to sit up and move away. Behind him, Tasha reached to the floor for the abandoned sheets and as he clicked on his cell phone he was sad to see her cover herself.

His sister responded immediately. "Junior, I'm so sorry. I didn't want to interrupt, but when I called Mom and Dad, they assumed you'd come and get me. You said your date was still hush-hush so I couldn't tell them...shit. I'm sorry."

Damn it, *no*. "Back up two paces, sis. Where are you, and why do you need a ride?"

"We went for coffee, Jamie and I, and I didn't feel like... Well, I convinced him to leave me there. But my car won't start, so I called Mom and Dad..."

And since he normally would have no problems coming to his sister's rescue, they'd immediately thought of him. "It's okay. Where you at?"

She told him, and even as he cursed his luck he was kind of grateful she'd had the sense to not go home with the guy. "I'll come and get you. Give me a few minutes. Oh, and phone Mom and Dad and tell them to stop calling me."

"I'm really sorry."

"Me too." He stared at Tasha. A frown marred her face, the bed sheet tucked under her arms. Her nipples poked against the front of the material and his body ached with the need to rip the thin fabric away and start all over again. "Later."

He hung up and groaned at the injustice of it. The woman of his dreams was in his bed, and he had to leave to rescue his sister. Life was hellish at times.

"Maxine needs a ride?" Tasha scooted to the edge of the bed. "Do you want me to go get her?"

He dropped beside her and pulled her back into his arms. "What I want is to have the phone never have been invented. I want to be making love with you, not doing a mercy drive."

There was no way to stop from kissing her, his hands automatically slipping under the sheet to caress her naked skin.

She pushed him away.

"Maxine will be waiting. You can't leave her alone out there."

He swore. "I know." He adjusted his cock, striving to find more room for the damn thing. He pulled on a T-shirt as he paced the room. Tasha's gaze followed him intently.

"Will you still be here when I get back?" he asked. *Oh God, you have to still be here.*

Tasha paused. "I should go home, Max. I hate to leave, but you have no idea when you'll get back. I don't want to make you rush. Deal with Maxine, and we'll talk tomorrow, okay?"

Fuck. Talking was not what was on his mind. "I could come to your place."

She nodded slowly.

He wasn't an idiot, not even with his brain fogged with lust. Somewhere in the last two minutes the whole thing had broken down. Between the passion that had flashed between them and the damn phone calls, she'd started thinking again, not in a good way. *Damn it all to hell.*

Dragging his brain back into working mode was rough. The raging fever in his body wanted nothing more than to order Maxine a taxi and spend the rest of the night in bed with Tasha. Yet, maybe—although his body thought he was an absolute idiot—maybe stopping before they went all the way wasn't a bad thing.

His body complained mightily—*it's a real bad thing.*

She'd said they were going to be friends only. He wanted more. Just because they'd started as friends didn't mean they had to remain that way. A frantic first rutting wasn't the kind of memory that would bring up romantic and heartwarming images, no matter how hot and bothered they both were.

Although he was convinced he was absolutely and totally insane even to suggest this.

He went for nonchalant. "How about we have lunch tomorrow? We can get all the details squared away that we have to. There's got to be some dating involved in this as well as everything else, right?"

The look of relief that crossed her face showed he'd made the right decision. "That's probably the easiest way to break it to the Turner clan without raising a ton of suspicion. Can we make it dinner? I have a full slate of projects tomorrow."

Max hurried back to her side for one last brief kiss, just to torment himself. The touch of her skin and her hair as he cupped the back of her neck in his hand made it even harder to leave. "Keep my keys. I've got another set. Lock up when you leave, and I'll call you in the morning."

Then he dragged himself from the room and out of the house, wondering what he'd done wrong to get the fates upset with him. Giving him his heart's desire and simultaneously wrapping him in chains.

Chapter Eight

Tasha was ready to kill someone.

More specifically, her friend, Lila. Maxine Turner was a close second, followed immediately by a whole myriad of Turners who popped to mind. It had been over a week since she'd agreed to Maxwell's proposal, and after that first abortive night together, their luck had gone from bad to downright impossible. Maxine had been the first to keep them apart—the first in a long line of interrupted attempts.

Max had sent her the sweetest note that next morning along with a single yellow rose. Something to the effect of not rushing things, making sure that they felt established as a couple within the family. It was the rose that said the most—he hadn't tried for anything other than friendship, and that helped to neatly tuck away a few fears.

The fears that had instantly flooded her mind when they'd been interrupted. Oh my God, the realization they were actually going to try to get her pregnant had hit hard enough to knock the lust right out of her. It was way more involved than simply hopping in the sack. If that's all it required, she would have called him over, jumped him, then sent him on his way immediately after. While she wanted to keep this as uncomplicated as possible, there was a much bigger reality to face. They were going to be together for a long time, and finding a way to make the whole relationship work...seemed like there had to be more than just giving into the physical attraction she would now admit she felt between them.

He was a great guy. Smart, honest. But the physical pull was there, and if he was in the same boat as her—he must be totally sexually frustrated. She'd at least gotten off that first night. Guilt rolled over her. He'd given her *two* orgasms already and not seen a bit of his own release. So much for all guys being selfish bastards—in this relationship it had been all her taking and him giving.

But every date they'd set up since his Gramma's party had ended in disaster. They'd begun to share the news that they were an item. While most of the clan hadn't raised a brow, they couldn't simply jump into bed without people wondering what was going on. This was still a small town, and slow and steady was the norm, at least for any lasting relationship.

She threw another dart, spearing into the spare piece of drywall she'd nabbed from the construction site and propped up as a way of releasing tension. Her aim was getting better all the time, especially as she'd dealt with a mass of anxiety this past week.

Enough. This wasn't acceptable. She couldn't get pregnant if they didn't have sex. They couldn't have sex if they didn't see each other. She picked up the phone and called him.

"At your service, my lady."

Didn't she wish? "You planning on bringing that servicing over here, big guy? I'm thinking some sex on the desk would be fine right about now."

Dead air greeted her from the other end of the line. Damn, the ease with which the explicit words slipped from her lips was proof again of how comfortable she was around him.

"Max? You okay?"

He growled at her. "No. I'm hard as a steel bat, and the images of bending you over your desk and fucking you silly are not helping the matter. I thought we agreed—I'm not taking you up against the wall or over the couch or on your desk our first time. Stop driving me insane, woman."

Holy shit. Yeah, that was descriptive enough to make her head spin and an ache start between her thighs. This was her fault for having sex on the brain. "Okay, now you've gone and done it. Thanks for getting my motor running when I just wanted to be nice and set up a date."

"My motor has been burning out on high for years, and we've had dates. Catastrophes, every one of them. Well, they've been great dates in the visiting department, but lousy in the sex department. You can't get pregnant having ice tea and fruit salad. Or through a telephone. Bell invented a great contraceptive."

She laughed. "Hey, you need to claim responsibility for half those disasters. The night I tried sleeping over at your place, I'm not the one who caved when the family showed up. An impromptu lawn party is one thing, but people deciding to stay and camp for the night kind of put a damper on things."

"You let Lila crash on your couch the night I was over..."

Shit. "I nearly revoked her BFF papers that night."

"Damn it, Tasha, this is insane. I think I had more opportunities for sex back when I was a teenager."

"Oh, so long ago, right?"

"Shut it." He laughed though, and something warm swept over her. The whole situation was ridiculous, but in spite of their no-show in the sex department, she was happy so far with her decision to let him into her life. Even now, getting to laugh with him over their frustrations—it boded well for the future. If they were going to raise a child together, getting along was

81

important.

"What are you up to today, Max? Shall we try for another date just to see what the Turner clan can come up with to keep us apart?"

Loud beeping noises filled the background, a door slammed and Maxwell sighed. "Ah, fuck it. I'm now officially hiding out. Someone from the manor house decided this week would be a good time for fixing the water main. There are backhoes and tractors in the side yard, all of them growling and making so much noise I'm never going to get any work done. I'm going to have to give up and hit a coffee shop to find some peace and quiet."

Tasha looked around her small office space. She'd rented a corner from a common work group until her new house was done and she could set up a proper home office. "I'd invite you to join me here, but there's barely enough room to swing a cat."

"Is there room to pet a pussy?"

She choked for a second. "Excuse me?"

"Damn it, Tasha, I'm dying. Are you wet? Did you get excited thinking about me coming over there and taking you on your desk?"

The answering pulse from between her legs was a resounding yes. "I thought you were going to a coffee shop?"

"I'm headed there right after I get rid of this wood. You want to help?"

Oh my God. Twenty-somethings were nothing if not blunt. "You said something about phones not making it easy to have sex. You figured out how to work instant teleportation?"

"No, but if you have any pity for me, you'll let me have some fun. Is the door closed to your office?"

She got up and closed it. Locked it. Put her landline on the answering machine. Hell, if nothing else, she owed him one. And if they were going to have phone sex, she wasn't letting anything interrupt them this time. "You need me to talk in a deep voice or something? Ask if you want to get dirty with me?"

He *hmmed.* "You can talk dirty to me, or you can tell me what you're doing. What are you wearing, Tasha? Skirt? Pants?"

"Skirt. Short one, with a thong underneath." He groaned and she didn't even fight the smile that rose to her lips. This was powerful and sexy, and she was ready to drive him mad. "I'm sitting in my chair, and I can put my legs up on my desk. You want me to do anything else? Shall I strip?"

"Leave the thong on. Play with your breasts first. You wearing your earphone?"

"Yup. Hands are both free. Actually, my hands are both full. Oh God, that feels good. I liked it the other night when you touched my breasts." She rubbed circles over herself, cupping and massaging slowly.

"Pinch your nipples. You've got a great set of tits, Tasha. I love how sensitive they are. How when I touched you, they tightened. When I suckled, your whole body quivered."

She reached under her blouse, shoving aside the fabric of her bra letting the base support her breasts from underneath and leaving her nipples free. "I wish you were here. Kissing me, sucking me. Biting—I like a little biting as well."

Tasha pinched harder and gasped with the shot of pleasure that raced through her. The cool air of the office space pooled over her bare skin, her breasts, her crotch.

"I'm going to fuck your tits sometime. I can picture it, pressing you around me, the head of my cock poking out and you licking it on every stroke. But that's only for fun for me, I don't think you get much out of that. I think you'd prefer if I fuck you the regular way."

She laughed. "What's the regular way?"

"How about this time with your heels propped on the desk and I come up between your thighs? I'll lean over your chair and hang onto the arms and pump into you hard. The chair will roll, so every time I plunge into you, I'll pull the chair back hard, so my cock goes deep."

Tasha dropped one hand to her sex, rubbing her clit through the layer of fabric covering it. "How are you going to do that when I'm still wearing this thong?"

The beeping noises in the background on his end grew louder again and he swore. "Bloody hell, what's a guy got to do to get a little privacy? Fuck it." There was a rustle, a few more swear words, a loud click, followed by the splash of running water.

"Max? What the hell is going on?" In spite of being extremely turned on, Tasha was highly amused.

"I'm in the shower. Damn workmen were right outside the bathroom and although I don't give a shit if guys want to watch me jerk off, there was a girl with them. I swear we've been cursed or something."

Hmm, payback time. "You're in the shower?"

"Dripping wet and naked, with my non-waterproof phone. If it shorts out... Well, we're used to frustration, aren't we?"

She could help deal with the aggravating interruptions, at least this time. It was too good an opportunity to resist. "I'm in the shower with you."

"I like that thought. Your wet skin rubbing mine."

"No. Well, maybe one rub, then I'm going down on my knees." He swore lightly, and she smiled, rubbing her clit harder, closing her eyes to picture it so she could describe enough to drive him wild. "I look up at you, the long length of your cock between me and your face. You're smiling."

"I'm fucking grinning my face off. What you going to do next?"

"Hmm, no this is all you. You're stroking your cock, squeezing it in your fist. The head has turned purple and there's a bit of liquid on the tip. I want to lick it but I can't reach, so you pull my head closer and hold yourself steady for me."

"Holy hell."

"I lick it off, and you taste so good I don't even tease you. I just open my mouth wide and suck you in. You're hot in my mouth, stretching my lips. I have to let you go to get you wet enough to be able to take you all the way."

The noises in the background picked up again, this time a slapping sound, and she pressed on her clit again. He was stroking himself, picturing her mouth surrounding him. She upped the ante.

"You want more. You press in so far you bump the back of my throat, but I can handle you. I swallow and you slip in even farther, until my nose is touching your abs. My mouth is full, and you taste good. A bit salty, but clean and sexy. And then you hold onto my head and pump your hips backs and forth like you're fucking my mouth and—"

"Damn..."

There was a loud crash, and the sound of water dancing against the bottom of the shower. Then the phone cut out and she laughed so hard she cried. By the time she could breathe again, the hard, aching tingle between her legs hadn't diminished a bit. She leaned back in her chair and pictured Max losing control in the shower, his seed spraying as he envisioned her mouth on him. She rubbed her clit until she came as well, a tight restless climax compared to when his mouth had been on her, but still satisfying.

Almost as satisfying as knowing she could make him lose control like that.

A harsh sweep of guilt caught up with her. This was supposed to be about making a baby. Just because she'd enjoyed how Maxwell moved in the bedroom didn't mean she should be playing with sex for sex's sake. Except—he was twenty-four, and no matter how much he insisted he wanted to get her pregnant, he had the libido of a twenty-four-year old.

She was damned if she did, and damned if she didn't.

No, they were going to have sex, and trying to convince Maxwell to keep it sterile and old-fashioned was never going to fly. He'd made that clear from their first explosive kiss back at the house. He needed this to be more than simply a duty—in fact... Tasha wandered her tiny office space, trying to make her tumbling thoughts come back into line. Maybe the whole fooling-around area was something she should make sure to do for him. After all, a steady sex life couldn't be a bad thing for a guy to look forward to. On the other side of the coin, there was no reason for her not to enjoy herself. She had always liked sex, as long as it was monogamous.

A cool pit opened in her belly. That was another reason to make sure she didn't stint on keeping Maxwell happy in the bedroom—if they ever made it there. She didn't want him to even consider looking elsewhere for a partner. A shiver of doubt crept in and she pushed it aside. No, being deserted for another woman wasn't part of this game plan. Been there, done that, burnt the T-shirt. That broken relationship had hurt enough she never wanted to have to experience it again.

Damn it all. The wonderful sensation she'd had floating through her after the phone conversation dissipated like weak bubbles.

She packed up her things. She already knew the afternoon was going to be a write-off and continuing to work was out of the question.

All her concerns piled up, jumbled together into a mess. Plotting about enjoying sex, her ongoing fears that she wasn't loveable, her guilt that by getting involved with Max she was cheating him out of experiencing love—because she didn't love him. Couldn't. It just wasn't...

Screw it. No way would she let her mind go there.

It was one thing to reason out her sexual game plan, another to completely to convince herself. If she could put aside her lingering concerns that having fun sexually with Maxwell was wrong, they might be able to get somewhere.

Somewhere in the next forty-eight hours she was determined to find a way to make this situation between her and Max move on to its logical conclusion. Because as enjoyable as the phone sex had been at the time, it wasn't what they needed to be doing.

She wasn't sure if she should be laughing or crying as she headed home.

It was four in the afternoon by the time Max completed his arrangements. He took one final look around the room before racing to his car and calling Tasha.

"You ready?" he asked.

There was laughter in her voice. "You survived! How nice to hear from you. I wasn't sure if I would need to find a new phone number for you or what."

"Damn phone is toast. Yes, I have a new one."

"Expensive phone call. Sorry about that."

He turned toward her apartment, on the lookout for potholes, nail strips—anything that might ruin tonight's planned activities. "It was worth every penny. I felt bad that I left you hanging."

"Oh, I took care of business myself."

Oh God, the images that rushed to his mind. His tongue slipped a few times before he could respond. "Was it good?"

"Adequate."

Shit. "I'll try to do better next time." As far as he was concerned, her orgasms were his responsibility from now on. Starting tonight. "Be ready in ten minutes. I'll be at your door. Leave your phone behind, and I'll do the same. The world will not fall apart if people can't find us for a few hours."

"Max? Where are we going?"

"Hey, people keep interrupting us, so I've decided the less anyone knows about what we're doing the better chance of success we have, right?"

"Good with me. I'll grab my purse and meet you downstairs."

Max disconnected the headset and tried to calm down. Damn, he was sitting in the car and his heart raced like he'd run the entire distance to her place. He pulled up to the curb and waited, deliberately not fidgeting with his fingers on the steering wheel.

Surely he had enough control to at least pretend to act like he was a grown-up.

Of course, that meant he got even more of a kick out of it when *she* snuck across the yard and into the car like a secret agent, pulling off her sunglasses with a flourish and removing a big floppy hat.

She gave him the biggest grin. "You telling me what we're

doing yet?"

"Nope, but put this in the glove box for me." He handed over his new cell phone and when she laughed, he had to join in. He made sure to drive carefully—all he needed was his uncle, who was one of the local cops, to pull him over. It would undoubtedly start an entire Turner clan chain reaction he desperately needed to avoid.

Whcn he pulled into the driveway at the construction site of her new home, she shook her head. "I still don't see the possibilities. Although I do have a few good memories of the place already."

"Me yelling at you?"

She laughed. "That ranks high on the list, trust me." She waited for him to come and open her door. "I know they've got the walls up, I was here two days ago, but there's nothing else. I guess we're picnicking on the floor."

Max nodded. "Would that be so bad? As long as we don't get interrupted?"

The expression on Tasha's face made the effort he'd gone through to get this ready worth all the sweat, and every penny. "I'll sit on the floor happily if we can have some time alone."

He unlocked the front door, opened it and gestured her in ahead of him.

Her gasp of surprise was music to his ears.

"Max, what in the hell?"

She went immediately to the table and chairs that sat in what would be the dining room. He'd bought the set he'd seen circled in the open catalog on the coffee table that night he'd tucked her drunken body into bed. Strange side effect of his eclectic memory—even in the midst of his sexual haze he'd noticed the advertisement and hoped it would be something to please her. Tasha ran one hand over the dark-brown iron chair backs, admiring the plush cushions, and when she twisted back toward him, a huge grin covered her face. "You goof. Lawn furniture inside the house?"

"It's as red-neck as I could get on short notice."

She laughed. "I don't know that we need the sun umbrella up, but it looks great. And the food? When did you have time to do this?"

He'd set the table, including candles and flowers. The bread was on the table already, the rest of the meal in the picnic cooler to the side. "Magic."

Then he pulled out a chair, and she smiled sweetly, kissing his cheek lightly before letting him seat her.

The sex between them might be a given, but he wanted to seduce her into so much more than insert tab A into slot B. In his mind, this wasn't about her getting pregnant; it was about becoming a family, and every chance he got, he was going to lay the foundation for that. Whatever reservations she had, he was confident enough for them both.

He lit the candles and reached for the food. Memory making, beginning now.

Chapter Nine

The salad was crisp, the pasta perfect. He'd gone out of his way and everything on the table was delicious, but it was the man at her side who commanded her attention. Tasha leaned back in her chair and examined him closely, his eyes and face animated as he shared an anecdote about one of the Turner camping trips. It was somewhere between an adventure camp and a horror story, and it wasn't so much the information he shared that made her smile, but the way he shared it.

Wholeheartedly. With all-out enthusiasm. Delight and love for his family shining through in every word. The thought of him turning that same energy on their own child thrilled her to death.

The man himself wasn't bad either.

The dark tinge in his hair hid most of the red highlights except when the candlelight danced over them. In his sister, the red color of the family was more noticeable. In Max, it gave a distinguished air to his neat trim, a bit of an extra shine that made her think of regal kings sitting in state on their thrones.

His biceps pressed the fabric of his dark button-down shirt taut, stretched over shoulders wide and strong. For a guy who filled his days with computer programming, she wasn't sure where he'd found the muscles.

"Are you working out?" she asked.

He took a sip of wine. "I wondered where you'd gone. You thinking about my body, are you?"

Tasha felt a blush race up her cheeks, but there was no denying it. Her earlier decision sprang to mind—this was allowed to be fun as well as a means to an end. She deliberately eyed him, daring to let her attraction show. "There's a lot to be admired."

Max reached for her fingers, linking their hands together. She thrilled at the sensual tingle that raced over her skin. "I do weights and I've been running. I also play tennis with my cousins and uncles when I have time."

"I didn't know you played tennis."

"I'm not a superstar, but I can return a few volleys. You play?"

She chuckled. "A little. I'd prefer to swim for a workout, or go for a run."

He trickled a finger up her arm. "We could try to run together. I know that doesn't always work, trying to match paces. But since you've got a fairly sedentary job as well, it might be good for us to get into some routines."

Oh, her favorite thing. *Not.* She made a face. "My downfall. Sticking to a routine isn't easy."

He adjusted his chair, moving closer to her side, and her heartbeat picked up. They'd been having a nice, calm conversation. What was he up to?

"You ready for some dessert?" He leaned over and stole a kiss before taking her plate and stacking it with his.

The brush of his lips teased, building the desire for more. "Depends. What's for dessert?"

He stared at her mouth for a second, then rose and cleared away the dishes. He vanished down the back hall for a moment before returning with two small containers. "I'm tempted to say you're for dessert, but I know you have a sweet tooth. Tonight, you get to indulge."

He cracked open one container, and she smelled the chocolate even before she spotted the dark brown sauce. "I'm supposed to be—"

"Eating healthy. I know. It's healthy. I won't tell you what's it in, but the recipe said it's got a third of the calories of a regular chocolate fondue, and there's no caffeine—don't ask me how. Enjoy."

The second container popped open to reveal slices of fruit. Max stabbed a strawberry onto his fork, swirled it in the dip then popped it into his mouth with a grin. "Hmmm. Of course, if you don't want any...?"

She had her fork in play before he could take another bite, her own strawberry dipped and in her mouth in a flash. She might be watching what she ate, but she was no fool.

Heavenly flavor danced over her taste buds and she moaned with delight. "Holy cow, this is amazing."

"You like?"

She leaned back in her chair and licked the chocolate off her lips, savoring every bit. "It's incredible. I've never had something that's healthy taste this good. You're a genius, Max."

"So I've been told."

In a flash, the temperature in the room flared from comfortable to heat-wave range. In spite of the tantalizing flavor tangoing with her taste buds, all her awareness was on him. Maxwell's gaze ate her up. The focused attention made her tingle—her skin, her breasts, her sex. He didn't play any of the erotic food games she'd read about. Didn't feed her, or twirl chocolate over her skin and lick it off. He might as well have, considering how excited she grew. Under his intent stare, she became much more aware of the sensual attraction between them. Every time she put the fork in her mouth, he responded—a moan or a small body movement—as if he was jealous of the tines as she licked them clean. Every time she swallowed, he swallowed in time with her. Something warned her the intimate connection growing between them was building to explosive levels.

Max enjoyed his own dessert, twirling the fork to gather the perfect amount of dip. The drive to have him drop the fork and twirl his fingers on her body instead increased. When he reached out and wiped a bit of chocolate from the corner of her mouth, she captured his finger. Her tongue wrapped around the digit, sweeping it clean, teasing it in small circles. Then she suckled lightly, thrilling when his pupils dilated. His brown eyes changed almost fully to black.

He pulled his hand away with a slight pop and a shudder shook him. When he spoke, the lust in his voice ratcheted up her desire another notch.

"I want you. No interruptions, no regrets."

She couldn't answer for a second, his need enveloping her like a cloud. It was past time for this. Reality reared its head for a moment. "I'm not trying to be funny, but...on the table?"

Max held out his hand to lead her to another part of the house. "I'm smarter than that..."

There was too much sexual tension between them to laugh when she saw he'd brought a mattress into the house. It lay on the floor of what would be the master bedroom. He'd piled it with soft quilts and pillows, and arranged a wild array of tea-light candles on boxes all along the perimeter of the room. He must have lit them before serving dessert. Tasha released her fingers from his and turned, intending to thank him for the thoughtfulness, but the patient man she'd had by her side all through the meal had vanished.

He kissed her madly, clutching her close. Biting her lips, nibbling on her neck and below her ear. She clung to him, fighting for balance. After kissing her breathless, he stripped off her top and bra, then stepped back.

Standing there, half-naked before him, the flickering candlelight dancing on her skin as his gaze raced over her made her suddenly uncertain. She wasn't sure what to do with her hands. She was no shy girl to cover herself, but the longer he stood there, staring, the more self-conscious she became.

Why the hell had she thought her thirty-four-year-old body would be enough to make this work?

"Max, is everything okay?"

He shook his head. "I can't believe we're here and this is happening." He laughed. "I can't believe someone isn't going to phone, or walk in, or do something to stop us."

Her insecurities vanished. He was as involved as she was, and just as nervous, it seemed. She lifted her chin and paced toward him, closing the distance. The floor was cold under her bare feet, the unfinished boards of the plywood rough and itchy as she reached for him.

"It's real. And no one will interrupt us."

She undid the top buttons of his shirt and leaned in to kiss his chest. He hauled her against him instead of letting her finish undressing him, the fabric of his jeans and shirt a high-texture contrast with her bare skin. Somehow between the kissing and the touching, he not only stripped off his clothes, he had them on the mattress with his naked body pressed over hers intimately.

Oh yes, this was worth waiting for, all her frustrations washed away by the pleasure of the contact. Tasha opened her legs wider, letting his hips fall between her thighs. Their tongues tangled, brushing rough sweeps against each other. She couldn't decide if she wanted to have him use that talented tongue on her body, or get straight to the good stuff.

He took control again, cupping both her breasts in his hands and pressing them together so he could suck and lap the tips until the electric sensation shooting into her core made her squirm.

She didn't want any more foreplay. Dinner had been enough. Heck, the past week had been enough, or maybe it was all the years leading up to this moment.

"Now, Max. I want you."

He rose, kissing his way along her collarbone, nibbling under her ear. She was ready to poke him, to tell him to hurry up, when she realized his shaft nudged her sex, slipping between the slick folds. Another slow rock, and another, rumbles of pleasure escaping his throat.

Then he lifted up on his elbows and looked her fully in the eyes as he pressed into her core.

They both groaned, Tasha from the stretching, the width of his shaft more than she'd had for a long time. Max held still, buried to the root in her body. He squeezed his eyes together and made the most hilarious face.

"You okay?" She ran her fingers through his hair and rocked her hips slightly.

"Don't move, or I'm going to lose it. Oh my God, you feel fucking fantastic around me."

Delight bubbled up inside her, along with a hint of mischief. "Like don't do this?"

She squeezed her inner muscles as hard as she could, reveling in the fullness. He cursed lightly and grimaced. "Witch. I mean it, I've never been in a woman bare before and no one warned me how good this would feel."

Tasha laughed. Her genius had obviously missed one line of study. "You'll survive. Now move, I need you to move."

Pleasure streaked his face as he pulled out slowly, then surged back in. The sensation of heat spread outward, each thrust drawing her climax closer and closer. Max reached down and pressed her right leg farther to the side. The angle of his penetration changed as he made contact with her clit, and she was the one to hiss in reaction.

The sounds of their bodies moving together echoed strangely off the unfinished walls, louder and more feral than usual. Wet noises, the grunts and groans that escaped their lips. The gasp of pleasure she made when he caught one of her nipples in his teeth and bit lightly on the tip. She was getting close when he froze, his cock jerking within her, heat expanding between them. He moaned her name with his release, and even having been denied her own orgasm, she couldn't help but smile.

She'd made him happy, and the thought of all those active swimmers on the loose—well, she didn't need to climax for them to work.

He lowered himself on top of her, kissing her face and sighing in her ear as he lay still for a minute. "Damn. Sorry, I was a little excited."

Tasha laughed lightly as she ran her fingers through his hair. Her body hovered on the edge of release, but she still wasn't too disappointed. "It's okay. I think the simultaneous climax thing takes practice."

Max shook his head. "Practice? I'm all for that. But in the meantime..."

He took her lips in a searing kiss before rising and giving her a sexier-than-sin smile. Then he made his way down her body, nibbling and kissing as he went. By the time he'd reached her sex she was back up to borderline ecstasy, ready to roll over the line with the slightest provocation. His tongue on her clit was more than enough, pleasure breaking in her core with a steady pulse. Tasha let the orgasm wash over her, taking away the tension of the past days, letting even her obsession with what this could be starting slip aside for a moment.

It's about making a baby.

But it wasn't. So she didn't protest when he returned up her level and rolled over, taking her with him. His cock nestled against her body, her torso draped over him.

"Give me a minute, and we'll start again."

Long slow strokes with his hands over her back followed as he kissed her, and she didn't mind a bit he'd been fast out of the gate. He scratched lightly, then rubbed small circles. A lazy sensation somewhere between pleasure and relaxation floated over her. The sexual tension faded slightly, at least until he cupped her ass and started playing. When he slid a finger along her cheek folds, a corresponding spark flared in her sex.

His touch was hot. Hotter than she'd expected, and she'd expected a lot. He lowered his hands to her hips and shifted her, and it was clear his erection was a lot bigger than she remembered it to be.

Ah, the energy of the young. "Damn that was quick."

"What can I say?" He suckled on her earlobe for a moment. "I've got a great motivator."

She was impressed, especially when she wiggled herself up to a sitting position and there was no doubt he was primed again.

He grinned. "Cocked and fully loaded."

"Cocky, you mean." Tasha lifted her hips and took him in,

moving slow enough to appreciate every inch of the firmness piercing her body. He reached up and helped lift her a few times before he got distracted. Both hands deserted her hips to enfold her breasts, their heavy weight making them sway as she moved in an easy rhythm.

Max growled, a sexy, needy sound, deep in his chest. "I'm gonna admit that I like these very much. You've got a great ass, Tasha, but your breasts have given me the dirtiest dreams for the longest time."

There was too much going on in her body to come up with a response. The sensations continued to build as she undulated over him. His fingers teased her skin, a light touch then harder. His smile lit up the room as he arched his hips, aligning her into position so he could pump upward easier. The speed of his motions increased, his cock pistoning in and out so fast she thought it might be the friction between them heating her up.

Max let out a rough grumble of pleasure, then slowed his pace.

He slid one hand away from her breast, abandoning it to reach between her legs. His thumb made contact with her clit and she squeaked involuntarily. Sensory overload approached as he kept up the pressure on her sensitive clit. He continued to drive his cock into her as his other hand teased her nipples.

Tasha closed her eyes and rode, letting the pleasure of all the different touches stroke her desire higher and higher until her climax burst out, shaking her body. Wave after wave brought her passage tight around his shaft. He slowed his hips, his rhythm broken into uneven thrusts that somehow drew out her orgasm, her sheath clutching his cock with each withdrawal.

Utterly spent, she lay over him, blood pounding through her system, but she wasn't allowed to relax into sleep. He flipped them again, this time withdrawing from her body, then pressing her to her belly and pulling her hips into the air. He was back inside her in an instant, her hips angled high as he thrust.

"Oh, that feels good." Tasha wiggled her hips, pivoting to take him better. He snuck a hand around her body and caught hold of her clit, rubbing in time with his thrusts. "Oh yeah, that feels really good."

The man was a machine. He pushed her into another climax in only a few minutes, the force of his thick cock plunging deep into her sex making it impossible to escape the pleasure coming to wipe her out. Euphoric pleasure made her giddy, and the tingling in her core had spread to her extremities. And he still didn't come.

"You're killing me," Tasha groaned. He'd turned her to her back, crawled between her legs, and was planting lazy kisses on the inside of her thighs.

"Nope. I'm finally getting what I've longed for. Besides, we've got all night."

"I didn't think we were going to have sex all night—Max!"

He licked everywhere. It took a concentrated effort to ignore the embarrassment factor and stop from squirming away. His tongue tickled her clit, descended along the side of her labia, crossed the divide to circle between her butt cheeks. If she weren't half boneless from her climax she'd have complained more. As it was, the noises of delight he made as he explored, the wet sounds of his tongue and his fingers against her nether lips, all of it made her hotter.

He spoke against her sex, kissing lightly between the words. "You are beautiful, everywhere. The way you look, the way you taste. I can't get enough of you." Another sweep, and she shivered. The temperatures outside had begun to drop, but the heat in here was just fine, thank you very much.

Suddenly, he was inside her again, hunger for more written in all his actions, his every touch. He started slow and gentle, then caught on fire, pounding into her body like a madman, driving in hard. The muscles in his shoulder and forearms bulged as he held himself over her. His hips surged forward, and she pressed her heels down into the mattress to meet him. There was no possible way she could be ready to climax so soon, but somehow, she was. He had played her body so well that this wild act was exactly what she needed to be able to rise back up one final time. Their bodies slammed together. Tasha waited for a single second to take her away. When it came, it was a lightning strike—hard, immediate. It exploded out in magnificent blast. Her core tightened and a harsh groan escaped his lips and Max rocked unsteadily, his face twisted in a grimace, this time one of ecstasy.

There was too much heat, too much pleasure, to do anything other than stay in one place and wait for the earth to settle. Her heart pounded, their breathing echoed harshly off the walls. Contentment filled her. Okay, that had been spectacular, no matter what ulterior reason they had.

Tasha wrapped her arms around him and pulled him on top, sweaty body to sweaty body. The cool air of the room hovered over them, but the heat they'd generated was more than enough to create an oasis to hide from the world.

He kissed her gently. "I'm extremely happy right now."

She pushed his hair back from his face and met his smile with one of her own.

"Me too." A yawn escaped, even as she whipped up a hand to try and hide it.

Max laughed quietly. "Did I wear you out?"

She nodded lazily. Why not admit it? "Is there a quilt to go along with this comfy mattress? I don't think I want to go home yet."

He rolled off her slowly, tugging her legs until she was curled up on her side. He reached over their heads and grabbed a quilt that he shook over them. One more twist let him nestle his body around her, bare skin against bare, his wet cock nestled in the seam of her butt. She was too relaxed to even think of finding a pair of undies to pull on.

This had been far better than the sterile setting of a medical room, and far more pleasurable. As a means to an end, she could handle sex with Maxwell. As a means to finding fun— with a friend? That was all it was. Right?

The tiny tea lights went out one by one as drafts caught them, or the wicks grew too short. The light coming in the window faded to nothing. Surrounding her was the warmth of his arms and the soft whisper of his words.

"You are home."

Chapter Ten

It was official. Maxwell Junior was officially head-over-heels in love.

He'd done his best to hide it from Tasha, and so far, he thought he had done a damn fine job. The shirt in his hands hung forgotten for a second as he wasted a moment regretting he wasn't simply allowed to let her know how he felt. Still, she accepted his attention and seemed to be enjoying his company—all good things that boded well for the future, right?

The drawer in front of him was finally empty and he moved to the next. Clothing and collected bits of junk got sorted, some tossed into the garbage, some into the box he was packing.

"You want me to save any of these dishes?" Tasha called from the other room. "Anything sentimental in here?"

You. You're the only thing in this house I need. He poked his head out of the bedroom and let the pleasure of seeing her wash over him again. "I picked most of them up at the thrift store when I finished college. Box them up and we can take them back there."

Tasha leaned on the table and raised a brow as she eyed him up and down. "Interesting packing attire. I'm not sure I want to know."

Max glanced down at himself and let out a snort. He was down to his boxers, and nothing else. "Yeah, unconventional, but it works. I figured if I was getting rid of old clothes, I should start with the T-shirt I was wearing. Then I realized that with all the dirt and dust bunnies I was unearthing, my shorts would just get messy—"

"The T-shirt you were wearing? There was nothing wrong with it. You didn't throw it out, did you?"

She crossed her arms and gave him this look that he totally couldn't interpret. He scrambled to explain. "It's got a tear under the arm. It's just one of my college shirts."

Tasha marched past him, brushing his body as she slipped into his room and grabbed the discarded garment from the edge of the box where it had caught when he threw it earlier. "There's nothing wrong with this shirt. You can't throw it out."

He laughed. "Okay, fine. You can have my ripped shirt." It would look far better on her than on him anyway. Especially if she wore it with nothing underneath, her long legs bare, her breasts pressing the front of the fabric—

Oh boy. He shook his head and willed his cock to behave. They needed to get the packing done sometime this century. The pile of his belongings grew smaller as he prepared to move in with her. He swallowed hard. Even the thought was enough to re-engage his cock. It was really happening, not only the sex with his dream girl, but the whole relationship and moving-in and establishing-a-family thing. For him, the most important thing in his world. Screw it if some people thought he was crazy, he'd been looking for this all his life.

She shook the shirt in his face. "Thank you, it's mine. You obviously haven't had as much practice as I have in making things last as long as possible. Since we're going to be roommates, you're going to have to make a few adjustments. Hey, do you think there's enough left in the fridge for lunch, or do we need to pick something up on the way to the lawyer's?"

"I'm easy." Max tried to make his shrug look nonchalant even as the roommates comment hit him hard. That's what she still thought of them as? *Damn*. He obviously needed to turn the romancing up a whole lot harder. Of course it hadn't been all that long since their first time together—two weeks in fact. Leaping forward into moving together had been Tasha's suggestion, and it still floored him.

He grabbed her by the hand and pulled her against him. "Thanks for letting me move in with you so quick. The thought makes my head spin."

"I'll admit it's a little weird to think about. I haven't shared a place with anyone for years. But it makes sense, even if the entire Turner family is ready and waiting to ask us all sorts of questions." She hesitated, then rested her arms around his shoulders as she played with the hair at the back of his neck. "Besides, you had a standing offer for this place, and my apartment is only a rental. Once the new house is officially done, we'll be moving again."

"You don't want to have to move twice, admit it."

He rolled his neck slightly, loving the glide of her fingers against his skin. She didn't seem to mind physical contact with him outside the bedroom, but there was still something missing. The spontaneity wasn't there yet, not on her part. Was it just the years she'd refused to see him as more than a friend? Had she gotten so good at turning him down she was now turning down what could be?

"Oh, I'm guilty of not wanting to move more than necessary. Hate it with a passion. In fact, I think I'll hire that part of the job to some of the Turner clan. That will get me back in their good books, right?"

"You're not in their bad books. It's going to take time for them all to catch up. Just because news travels through the extended family like wildfire, doesn't mean they take it in that fast. Look at my folks—they're totally fine with the whole situation."

"Your parents are incredible. I was sure they would at least give me a few dirty looks when they found out we were moving in together."

"They are cool—but you gotta realize they've learned there's no use arguing with me. I'm a grown-up, and I've proved enough times I can take care of myself. Besides, they like you. Always have."

He swayed from side to side, enjoying the feel of his arms around her. They'd been making love daily for the past couple weeks, and he couldn't get enough of touching her. They'd talked a ton as well, figuring out the details of the prenatal arrangement. He'd been careful to avoid anything like making a promise to keep things nonemotional, and nothing but "friends only forever". He wasn't about to lie, but he wasn't about to scare her away.

He'd practice the fine art of the slow seduction of her heart and cross his fingers that no matter how much she said she only wanted a friend, that eventually she'd accept him as much more.

"We still need to let everyone know we're getting hitched. What time did the ceremony finally get set for?"

She stiffened for a split second before returning to cuddle against him. "Sorry, that still freaks me out. We've got an appointment for a week from Friday, at two."

He kissed the top of her head. "Freaks me out a bit as well, if it makes you feel better."

"We could wait until—"

"We're not waiting, Tasha. This is important to me. We're having sex and you could be pregnant already. I want to be married before I hear I'm going to become a father. Maybe that makes me some kind of weird toss-back, but you'll just have to put up with my old-fashioned ways."

She stretched up on her toes and kissed his nose. "You know what? That's very sweet, and I promised I would marry you, but I'm saying there's no rush because I don't feel like I'm pregnant."

Oh? "You have some mystical crystal ball you're consulting, or did you get your period?"

A gasp escaped her. "Umm, that's blunt."

He snickered softly. "I thought you were used to it."

Her cheeks flushed to bright red, and she wouldn't meet his eyes. "I'm not talking about my period with you."

"Bullshit. We've been over this. You want to get pregnant, we need to talk about it. I thought you were going to make me a chart? I know you've got one. You've probably been tracking for months."

"Jesus, do you know how weird this is? To talk about my period with a guy? Yes, I've got a chart, but you don't need to be studying it or anything. Just...have sex with me. That's enough."

Max debated which way to take this. She'd been fighting to maintain control in the strangest of areas. Maybe straight-out logic would be best. "Is your cycle twenty-four days? Longer? Shorter?"

"Max!"

Of course, teasing was good as well. "Hey, I'm up on basal temperature and all that stuff as well. I'll take your temperature every day if that will help."

She shook with her laughter now. "You, Maxwell Turner, are not a normal male."

"So I've been told. But since we're trying to get preggo, I figured I should do some research. For example, in the book *What to Expect When You're—*"

She peeled out of his arms and sat on the edge of the bed, holding her stomach and laughing. "You've started reading baby books? Oh my God, you're a brave man."

"No, brave is when I ask if you've got PMS and don't run to hide the knives."

A loud shout burst from her. "Now you're looking for trouble."

"I think I found it." He stepped on either side of her legs.

Tasha stared up at him. "You confuse me."

He grinned back. "You make me hot."

Neither of them seemed to be able to stop smiling and inside, he cheered. She seemed to have forgotten temporarily that she wasn't interested in being more than friends. "You ass, is that going to be your standard answer when you want to win a fight?"

"Don't see why not. It's true, and it works." Besides, it made her flush slightly every time he said it, and he was willing to use every weapon in his arsenal to get the upper hand. After flicking a glance at his watch, a happy idea overtook him. He pressed her back on his bed and buried his face between her breasts. In spite of having spent the morning packing, she smelled wonderful, a hint of jasmine rising on the air.

They'd been apart for far too long, at least twelve hours. "So..."

She wiggled under his touch. "So...what?"

"Are you, or aren't you? Because we totally have enough time for a quickie, if you're not having your period..."

She wasn't, and they did, and he'd never been happier.

Rolling with her on the bed in the midst of his college paraphernalia, it was like a homecoming and a hint at the future. Tasha seemed very willing to acknowledge the physical chemistry between them. Max wanted much more. The much more he was determined to achieve, one step at time, and luckily for both of them, each step was turning out to be very pleasurable.

"You've got to be kidding. I swear this is some kind of elaborate hoax you two have concocted."

Tasha sighed into her teacup. Of all the people to have trouble with her situation, she didn't expect Lila to be the one to freak so hard. Yeah, there had been a few warning grumbles when Tasha had shared that she and Max were dating, but she'd thought that was just from the initial surprise. Heaven knew Lila had heard her complain often enough over the past year that having a man in her life was a low priority.

Now that Saturday had rolled around it was less than a week before she and Max were supposed to make it official. She'd finally got up the courage to drop by Lila's place and tell her their plans. "No, I'm not kidding. Max and I are getting married."

"You can't marry him!"

She raised a brow at her friend's bold declaration. "I can't? Why? Is he married already, with a passel of kids I don't know about?"

Lila growled at her, leaning back in her chair and folding her arms. "If you're not going to be serious about this..."

"I am being serious. Max and I have decided to get married. I want you to come and be one of our witnesses. It's at two o'clock. Are you free?"

"You've been turning the boy down for dates for years, and now you're not only dating, you're getting married? Jumping the gun or what?"

Tasha sighed. Yeah, the tough questions were starting already, and she had only a few options. Either she told the plain and simple truth to Lila, or she lied her head off and pretended to be madly in love. She didn't want to confess about the baby making to anyone—not even Lila. That topic was something that down the road neither she nor Max wanted trotted out at a Turner gathering. A bold-faced lie was also out of the question. Lila would never in a million years believe her to have fallen head over heels so fast.

Max had suggested a middle ground, and she'd thought it was a good idea. Unfortunately, Lila wasn't buying.

"He's not a boy anymore, as he very eloquently pointed out. When I finally agreed to date him, I realized we clicked. It doesn't make any sense to wait around and make it a long drawn-out engagement and stuff. We've known each other for ten years."

Lila wrinkled her nose. "Please, he was underage for most of that time."

"You know nothing sexual happened back then."

Her friend shook her head. "I don't understand you. From wanting nothing to do with the Y chromosome to committing to marriage?" Lila narrowed her eyes. "You're up to something, and I'm not sure why you're not telling me the truth. You've had your damn head in the clouds for months. I figured it was stuff with your work or the house-building project. Now you want me to believe you've fallen in love with my cousin and that's it?"

"Why is it so hard to believe?" Tasha scrambled a bit. Having to convince Lila was not on her list of things to do. She'd known it was a stretch—to hope for a quiet coffee break, a congratulatory hug, and then back on her way into a full day that included way too much work. While she and Max were keeping the wedding small and strictly businesslike, there still seemed to be a million things to do.

The fact she'd gotten her period that morning hadn't added any joy to the day either. The complication of having to win over her friend seemed a little too much to take at the moment. "It's happening. It's real. I just want you to be happy for me."

"I can't condone this." Lila glared at her. "He's my freaking younger cousin, barely out of his teens."

Tasha covered her wince as best she could. This was not going to be easy, not with Lila shooting back all the concerns she thought she'd finally convinced herself weren't issues. Now she got to try saying her responses out loud, like she meant them. She hoped they sounded as convincing this time around as they had when she'd jumped into the relationship with Max.

"Oh, bullshit, you know he's not a teen. He's twenty-four, and he's more mature than most of the thirty-year-olds we've been dating. If you pull off the blinders, you'd have to admit that he's an adult, and a great guy."

"There's no way I'm admitting anything. This is simply way too weird."

Damn it all. "Look, we're not asking for your permission, I'm asking if you want to be my witness—"

"I'm sorry, but I don't see why you're doing this. Unless you guys had sex and you got knocked up or something, I see no reason for you to get married. Hell, even if that's the case, I still see no reason for you to get married."

The streak of pain that flashed through Tasha was real, and made her angry all over again. There was no way someone who wasn't longing for a child could understand how much it hurt to have to spit out the words. "I'm not pregnant."

"What the hell is going on then? And why aren't you telling me the truth? I mean, one minute you're sworn off guys and the next you're getting married? How come I didn't hear a word about your change of heart before now?"

Shit. "I just..."

"Just what? Didn't think you could tell me? Didn't think you should talk to someone before you made a life-changing decision?"

Tasha froze, her fingers clutching the edge of her cup. It was true. She hadn't told Lila, not a word, about her plans for artificial insemination. All through the debating and questions, she'd clutched the idea tightly to herself and kept it a secret. Why hadn't she disclosed her thoughts to Lila? The question had bothered her until she'd realized she didn't want to tell out of fear Lila would try to talk her out of it.

Lila had always acted like she was the voice of reason, stilling many of the exciting new adventures Tasha wanted to try. Coaxing her back to far more ordinary paths. Some of the time Tasha was grateful, but there were times that she'd wondered if the safe route Lila insisted on was really the one to take.

Like she was trying to talk her out of this now.

Was she correct in this circumstance? Maybe, but it was still Tasha's decision. Somehow, she needed to get that across.

She blew out a long slow breath. "I'm sorry. I have been keeping secrets, but I think this is what I need to do."

"How can it be the right thing? Tash—you're way older than him. You're settled in your life. You've got everything you need. Why throw it away and make this kind of radical change?"

Tasha frowned. *What the hell?* "At thirty-four I'm settled? I'm not supposed to change or grow from here on? That doesn't make any sense. There's a whole lot of life in front of us still,

Lila, and I never planned on staying stagnant. I know it seems like a stretch, but can you trust me? I've given it a ton of thought and—"

Lila rose to her feet, disgust written on her face. "Jesus, I didn't know you were so desperate for a guy that you had to go cradle robbing. Don't do this. You're making a huge mistake."

Tasha fought the tears that threatened. "Never in a million years did I expect you to respond like this."

"Never in a million years did I expect you to go trolling through my family to find—"

"Enough!" Holy shit, where had this gone so wrong, so fast? Tasha stood and grabbed her purse, swinging it over her shoulder and stiffening her spine. "I'm sorry this upset you. That wasn't my intention."

Lila shook her head. "Then stop what you're doing and listen for a minute. You don't need to go racing off into marriage. Just...put it on the back burner for a while. Tell Max you need more time. You and I can take a holiday. Plan some fun things to do together. I don't know, maybe some retail therapy. A bunch of girls' time out and you'll be able to see things in a clearer light."

Fuck. She wasn't getting it. "What light is that, Lila?"

Her friend rounded the table, as if coming in for a hug. "You need something to get you back to normal."

A laugh burst out, shaky around the edges. Tasha backed away. Lila didn't understand, and she was talking crazy-talk. Shopping was supposed to be an alternative to getting married? "Normal? What's normal? Hanging out with you and—?"

"Yes. There's nothing wrong with that. Nothing wrong with how things were going in our lives before you decided you needed a guy around again. It's not worth it, Tasha. Just give up trying to find that kind of happiness, okay?"

Tasha closed her eyes for a second and prayed for strength. "You don't understand."

"No, I don't, and if you insist on going ahead with this stupidity, you're on your own. I won't be a party to it." Lila's arms were folded again, red flushing her cheeks.

"I take that as a no to witnessing then."

"Damn straight."

She waited for one more second, hoping that there would be some sign of weakening. Something that she could say to redeem this fuck-fest of a conversation. Nothing. Lila turned her back and slipped into the kitchen.

Tasha forced herself to walk calmly away, wondering if this was indicative of what she could expect in the days to come. So much for the entire Turner family being supportive and welcoming. Her friend had not only dismissed her and Max as a couple, but reawakened everything she'd worried about in terms of a long-term relationship with him.

What the hell had she done?

She escaped into her car before she gave into her tears, indulging for a moment. There wasn't anything more she could do about Lila, but it hurt.

Damn hormones anyway. Getting her period hadn't helped the situation either.

Her phone rang and she cleared her throat carefully before answering it.

"Hey, Max, what's up?"

His voice sounded light and happy on the line. "I was wondering how it went with Lila. Does she need a ride or anything to the office for Friday?"

So much for having a clear throat. Her response stuck. "She's not coming."

"Damn, that's too bad. I was worried with it being short notice people might have trouble. Did she already have a commitment?"

Tasha leaned her head on the cool glass of her side window. "She thinks I'm an idiot and cradle-robber. She does not approve of us getting married, and I think she hates me a little right now."

"No way. Are you kidding? Lila would never hate you."

"Yeah, well, she's not coming."

"Oh, Tasha, I'm so sorry."

"Me too." They sat in silence for a minute.

He coughed, his voice gentle when he spoke again. "I'm not sure if this is the right time, but I actually called because someone had something they wanted to say to you. Are you okay if I put them on? I think...you might like to hear this."

Right now? All she wanted to do was crawl back into bed and pull the covers over her head. "Fine."

"Hey," he whispered, "it's going to be okay, all right?"

She sighed.

Suddenly her ear was filled with a long, loud squeal of delight. "Oh my word, Tasha, are you guys serious? You're getting married? That is so fantastic, I swear I'm shaking."

If a phone could produce bubbles, she'd have been buried in a flash, the sheer enthusiasm and excitement pouring over the line sending tiny smacks of refreshment against her weary soul. "Maxine?"

"I'm sorry, I should have said it was me. Junior just told me, and asked if I'd come and witness, along with Mom and Dad, and I'm so excited for you guys. This is perfect. I've been telling Max for years to get his butt in gear and stop farting around, and ask you out again, and now you're not just dating, you're getting married? I'm so happy for you."

Tasha clung to the phone, not sure what to say. Which didn't seem to matter because Max's sister seemed to have enough to say for the both of them.

"I know you want to keep it pretty low-key and all, and I guess I can see that. I mean, a Turner wedding? Insanity times ten. But can I at least convince you to take some spa time with me on Thursday? Did you pick out what you're going to wear yet? Oh my, what about some flowers—let me take care of that, okay? And if you'd like, I'll ask Maxamin to come and take a few pictures. He'll be happy to, and that way you can still have something to flash for the clan when they all ask."

Tasha forced herself to cut in before the bubbly outburst continued for too long. "So...you're okay with the idea of Max and I getting married?"

"Are you crazy? I think it's awesome. Tasha, you've been around forever, and you guys fit perfect, really. Only I'm a little choked that I didn't notice that you were dating. He only told me the night of Gramma's party, and I thought that was like your first date. You guys have been sneaky, but I don't care too much. It's your life, and again, that whole Turner thing... Secrets can be a good thing."

A short laugh escaped Tasha, the tightness in her chest easing. "Maxy, I can't tell you how much this means to me. I'm touched."

"You're touched? I'm going to have a sister! I'm over the moon. It may seem like I've got people around all the time, what with the clan and everyone, but you're special. You've always been special."

Damn it, the girl was going to have her in tears again without even trying. "I'm very glad you're pleased. Thank you for being willing to witness for us. And the pictures sound like a great idea. The spa as well."

"Do you have a dress picked out? Can I help with that?"

A dress? Pictures, a spa trip? She'd planned to wear a nice suit she had and figured that would be enough. Suddenly, it wasn't, and all of Maxine's enthusiasm helped to ease the pain of Lila's rejection. It didn't wipe it away completely, but it was certainly a step in the right direction.

"I don't want anything too fancy, but yeah, if you'd like to go shopping with me, we can do that. Monday?"

Maxine gushed a bit more before setting up a time and place to meet, and passing the phone back to her brother. Tasha's thoughts spun as she considered what to say to him. Somehow in one move he'd accomplished the impossible, without even trying.

"Tasha?"

"You have the sweetest sister in the world, you know that?"

He chuckled. "I seem to have told her that a few times. She argues with me, but the proof is all there." His voice dropped a notch. "You all right? I'll be done my to-do list in about an hour, then I can join you."

"You're nearly done already? How the hell did you do that?" They'd split the list of things they had to accomplish, and she'd done...none of hers, since number one had been to get her witness lined up.

"Efficient task planning, and a whole lot of bullying my relatives into favors. Tell you what. Go home. I'll meet you there. If I help you with your stuff, we'll be done in no time. Also, if you're okay with it, my parents wanted to have us over for a celebratory dinner."

"That sounds...like just what I needed to hear." She paused for a second. "Hey, Max?"

"Yeah?"

She could picture him, that flirty smile on his face, his eyes attentive and bright as he waited for her. "Thanks. I'm going to be okay."

"We're going to be more than okay, but it will take time. I'll catch you in a bit."

She hung up and stared out the window. There were a few clouds floating against the brilliant blue sky, but for the most part, it was clear and bright. She wasn't crazy, she had to trust that the situation with Lila was merely a cloud passing in front of the sun for a brief moment.

She turned and headed home, surprised, but pleased to be looking forward to Maxwell's company for the rest of the day. It made the bitter a little easier to deal with.

Chapter Eleven

Max had a difficult time remembering to keep it light. From the moment he'd picked up Tasha from his sister's where she'd been getting ready for the ceremony, he'd been fighting to hold back the sweet words that wanted to escape.

It was much more than she made him dizzy with lust. The fact she trusted him enough to tie her life to his without loving him—that appealed to him more than she could possibly know. He knew what he felt, and how it motivated him to want to give everything to her. She on the other hand, was going into this based strictly on logic, and somehow that impressed him more than if she had confessed her undying love.

Although he really wanted that as well.

Now she stood across from him, repeating the simple words they'd written together. Promises to be there for each other, and for their family when one came along. He grinned harder, remembering how smug Tasha had seemed that she'd managed to successfully avoid using the word *love* in their vows.

What was love, but a commitment? He hoped he'd be able to rub that in sometime during their first anniversary.

Having his sister there was sweet, and bitter, considering Lila had refused to reconsider and continued to give Tasha the cold shoulder. He couldn't see how his cousin could be so self-centered and stubborn, especially after he'd called her to try and talk sense into her.

They finished the simple ceremony, kissed Maxine and his parents farewell, and ducked into his car.

"Are you finally going to tell me where we're going?" Tasha undid her sandals, leaned back in the car seat and propped her feet up on the dash. He swallowed hard at the sight of her legs extending from under the pale purple of her dress. "I assume it's not back to the apartment, since you insisted I pack an overnight bag. You know, we didn't need a weekend away."

Max pulled onto the highway, hoping he hadn't pushed it too far, but there was no way he was going to let their honeymoon weekend be back at her apartment, doing ordinary everyday things. He was intent on making memories, secret though it be for now. He gave her the explanation he'd prepped.

"My parents wanted to give us something."

"That's sweet, but they didn't need to."

He nodded. "I know, and I told them that. But since we already have all the house stuff we need, and we said we didn't want them to host a luncheon or anything, they insisted. The only other thing I could come up with that worked was a booking at an oceanfront cabin. It made them happy, and I thought it would suit our plans. We can talk about some of those habits we want to get into, and the beach is a great place for long walks and workouts. And, there's no junk food there."

Natasha didn't say anything for a bit, and he thought he heard the gears spinning in her brain. "That sounds...great."

"I'm also planning on having lots of uninterrupted sex."

She laughed. "No ulterior motive on your part to hide us away, was there?"

"Just because we're now officially a couple doesn't mean the Turner clan will cease to exercise their uncanny ability to interrupt us. In fact, over the next while we'll probably have to run the gamut, with every one of the individual families inviting us over for celebratory coffee and cake, and what have you. Rejoice in your final moments of relative freedom from the excesses of relatives."

Tasha's smile faded. "Not everyone is celebrating."

She turned to look out the window, and he sighed. *Damn Lila.* He reached over and grabbed Tasha's fingers, ignoring her surprised response. He nudged up the music volume, discouraging talk and letting the miles pass as they sat in silence. He wasn't going to try to fight the hurt her friend's disapproval had caused, and unless Tasha decided to get mad and tell Lila to grow up, he was trapped. At least until he had a little more time on his hands.

His best offense at the moment was to ignore Lila and hope she came around soon.

It was only an hour's drive to the cabin, and he smiled in anticipation. He'd come here a few times before, once with the guys for a Turner Boys Weekend out, and once by himself when he was trying to figure out what he wanted to do before his final year of college concluded. He'd never imagined that he'd be returning with a wife.

Tasha stretched, her arms pressing against the roof, sending her breasts tighter against the scooped neckline of her dress. His cock stirred and he adjusted himself.

She laughed. "You're certainly not shy."

For a second he couldn't figure out what she was talking about. A quick glance and her pointed stare at his groin cleared up that mystery. "Anytime you want to help me, I'm game. You have no idea what it's doing to me, seeing you in that frilly dress and longing to see if you actually wore the garter I sent you."

"Your sister is extraordinarily bossy for a sweet and quiet girl. Of course I'm wearing it."

Hot damn. "Show me."

She jerked in her seat. "Now?"

He forced his eyes back on the road. "I'm curious, that's all."

Tasha sat motionless for a minute, before pushing her seat back as far as possible. She shimmied her hips lower, then slowly inched the hemline toward her hips. In his peripheral vision, the details blurred together, the only thing clear the decreasing amount of purple and the increasing expanse of bare skin. The warning for their off-ramp passed, and he gratefully took the curve, turning onto the side road toward the cottage a touch too fast. His tires squealed and Tasha tsked.

"If you can't pay attention to the road, I'm going to have to stop."

Oh my God, no. "Totally in control here, honestly. That's a very tight corner."

"Hmm, I see." Her cool fingers reached over and grasped his right hand, pulling it off the wheel and lowering it carefully to her thigh. Under his palm, her flesh was warm and soft, and he swore lightly. When she tugged his hand closer to her crotch, letting him find the garter, he knew he was in for a world of pain before he got any relief.

"If I can mention, you've made my cock hard."

"I noticed. That's not a bad thing."

He slipped a finger under the elastic, trailing back and forth along the lacey edge. The smooth swell of her inner thigh teased him, and he snuck farther toward her center.

When he met nothing but smooth, bare skin, the steering wheel jerked before he got the car under control. He whipped his hand back and carefully resumed hanging on to the ten and two position with a death grip. That was as far as his control could go. He couldn't change his harsh breathing that sounded as if he'd just finished running a marathon. And he certainly couldn't stop his arousal from pressing against the front of his slacks.

"Umm, that was supposed to be a surprise for... later."

The images flashing through his mind were far too vivid. "Please tell me you mean five-minutes-from-now later, not five hours from now."

"Where's the cottage?" Lust painted her tones and his anticipation rose.

The pavement ended as he turned into the entrance, the car bouncing a little too hard over the rough driveway before he slammed to a stop in the rustic single parking space. They were at the far end of a row of tiny cabins, tight up against the rocky precipice of the cliffs. He had the car turned off and was at her door in record time, but she still beat him. Tasha stretched again, arms reaching overhead as she dragged a deep breath of salty sea air into her lungs. Her bare feet dug into the sand, the filmy layers of the skirt of her dress fluttering around her knees in the light breeze off the ocean.

He caught her by the back of the neck and hauled her lips against his, bodies instantly in full contact. She joined in willingly, wrapping her arms around him and opening her mouth to his assault. He couldn't slow down, not this time. All the tension that she'd built unwittingly since he'd first spotted her in that pixie-like dress—damn it, he wanted relief, and he wanted it now.

Luckily, it seemed she had the same idea. As they kissed, lips hard against each other, she tugged him with her as she backed up until she'd trapped herself between the hood of the car and his aching groin. A quick hop put her on the surface, her thighs spread wide to allow him to stay in intimate contact with her. His hands came down on the hood to check the temperature, but the surface was warm, not boiling hot. The hottest thing was her, the way she rubbed against him, the way she participated in the steamy kiss.

When he finally dragged his lips away he was shaking. "Tasha, I can wait two more minutes—"

"I can't."

She undid the buttons of her dress top faster than he thought possible, revealing another purplish article of lingerie. The fabric was so sheer her nipples showed through, the darker circles poking the fabric like tiny mountain peaks in the middle of rosy plains. She dropped a hand between her breasts, twisted her fingers, and the cups popped apart leaving the heavy globes bare to the sunshine and his adoring gaze.

He doubted his cock could get any harder. Except—it did. When she grabbed his head and pulled him to her, lining up a nipple with his lips, all bets were off. There could be an audience watching and he really didn't give a shit. He lapped once in a circle then enveloped the tip, sucking hard. Tasha cried out and adjusted her position, arching her back to press her breast farther into his mouth. He switched sides, letting the moisture from his mouth leave one tip glistening in the sunshine before changing back to the other.

Tasha propped her left foot up on the hood beside her hip, leaned forward and reached for his belt. Even as their mouths reconnected she managed to open his pants and slip her hand in, grab his erection and pull it free. She stroked him, and it felt so damn good. Not that she needed to prime him anymore, but with every pass she trailed her thumb over the head, smearing the precome over the tip. He let it go on until he felt his balls drawing up. Too fast. Too out of control. He was seventeen again and jerking off to the thought of her touch, and now she was touching him and he had no more control than back then. He pulled away and dragged his gaze up off her magnificent tits to stare into her eyes.

Sheer mischief reflected back as she leered at him. "Do I make you hot?"

"Wench."

He rearranged her slightly, shifting her to the side, allowing enough room for him to place her right foot up on the hood as well. The scoop of her dress fell to hide her sex. She leaned back on her arms, forcing the open buttons on top to spread wide around her breasts like some kind of erotic postcard. He placed both palms against the sides of her full rounds, pressing and lifting them together, admiring her as she shook her head and let her dark hair fall around her shoulders.

He placed his hands on her knees, slipping upward, over her thighs, dragging the fabric away to reveal her bare mound. His cock jerked where it stuck out from his pants. Liquid glistened on her labia and he traced a finger slowly through her folds and she shuddered.

He pressed in, never looking away as she enclosed him in her moist heat. Tasha purred, wiggling her hips closer to the edge of the car hood, pressing against him. He pulled out slowly, the moisture painting his finger drawing him like a magnet. He brought his hand to his mouth and licked away the cream, groaning as the taste of her hit his tongue.

"That's so wicked." Tasha whispered the words and he smiled at her.

"We're about to have sex outdoors and you think that's wicked? Watch. Watch every fucking second."

He stepped forward, opening her with one hand, running

his thumb over her labia gently. One movement lined up the ready head of his shaft and he slowly let her surround him, the sight making the sensations that much more powerful. Tasha moaned softly, bringing down a hand to touch where they connected.

Her finger running along the seam between his cock and her opening nearly undid him.

"I can't last longer than thirty seconds around you." Max ground the words out through gritted teeth.

"I can't either. Damn, that looks incredible. Now fuck me."

He did.

Max grabbed her hips and pounded into her, his cock disappearing between her folds to reappear, shining in the sunlight. Erotic as all get-out. She'd been primed on the ride out, hell she'd been hot since she'd gotten herself waxed and lady-scaped. A full Brazilian had never been in her plans before, but she'd thought he'd like it. Seeing him join with her, out of doors, where anyone going by could watch?

If she got any more turned on she'd spontaneously combust. She'd never known she had a streak of exhibitionism.

Then he ducked his head between them and latched onto one of her nipples, biting lightly, and she came. Pulses of pleasure shook her core, surprising her silly since she fully expected to need clitoral stimulation to climax. He didn't stop when she called out her pleasure, driving in repetitively until she felt a renewed electric tingle.

"Oh God, again." She grabbed his shoulders, pressing her knees wider to the side. He leaned over her, plunging downward more. The change in angle dragged his shaft along her clit on each move, and she couldn't help groaning. The sunshine, the gentle touch of the wind against her skin, the wordless grunts from his lips as he thrust. All of it combined together into one exquisite blend of sound and sensation and when she came this time, he joined her, his forehead resting against her shoulder as he shook with his release.

They sat like that for a full minute—an obscenely erotic figurine perched on the hood of his car. Then his shoulders shook again, and she leaned back to catch a glimpse of his face. He wore a grin that lit up his face and made her smile as well.

"You look pleased with yourself."

Max kissed her gently before slowly detaching himself. A rush of semen followed and he jerked off his shirt to wipe her clean, managing to keep her pretty dress from being stained. She was surrounded and petted, his hands smoothing everything back into place, lowering her gently to the ground. Holding her against his bare chest. Her fingers found their way to him, touching him slowly as he swept her up and carried her into the cabin.

She'd been very happy to take the step of the actual wedding and put it behind her. And although the idea of a honeymoon made something inside her cringe, what he'd offered was just fine. A chance to enjoy each other's company, away from the Turner love/hate relationship she was developing. As a background for raising a child? Fabulous. For the rest of it? Well, they'd be setting up some firm boundaries regarding the Turners and their personal relationship, if she had any say. Not only had it been tough to get together in the first place, she wasn't sure she could handle any more responses like Lila's. Maybe if they got some space for a bit—and then the damn guilt hit her again and she knew she'd never try to come between Max and his family.

She couldn't. Wouldn't do that.

The rest of the weekend passed in a pleasant blur as they

walked the beach, ate simple meals and planned for the future. The sex they shared was frequent enough to please her pregnancy plans, and to keep Maxwell grinning most of the time.

They had already dealt with all the legal implications of joining their households. Health insurance, a combined account to deal with family expenses. The rest of their finances and investments were still in their own names. Tasha'd been floored to find out exactly how much Max was worth. It didn't seem right that someone in their twenties had more stashed away than she did, and she'd been living frugally.

He'd laughed when she teasingly complained he must have found a gold mine.

"You didn't get into the computer stuff I did at the right time. Plus, I fooled around with a few projects while I was in college that made me a bit of cash." Max leaned back in his Adirondack chair, the full light of sunset shining on them as they relaxed on the porch.

She sipped her ice tea and admired the view. "You amaze me. All those years when we met at various Turner events it never registered that you were actually done with high school, then you were done with college and working for yourself."

He laughed. "That was deliberate. It was bad enough I was fourteen when I finished high school. When Mom and Dad let me challenge the college entrance exams, they didn't expect me to get in. Then I don't think they expected me to survive the rest of the semester when my classmates were all so much older."

"Wasn't that weird? Being the youngest all the time?"

He shrugged lightly. "When we were in class, there were no troubles. My lab partners didn't care about my age, as long I knew how to calculate formulas. Outside of college time? I hit my growth spurt early enough I was simply a tall, skinny guy. I didn't try to fit in with the crowd that was dating and fooling around at the bars, since I couldn't get in anyway."

He raised his glass mockingly and she laughed. "Oh God, I'd forgotten that part. No wild Spring Break parties then?"

"Didn't miss it. I found enough other people who were interested in games, and that was pretty much how I passed what spare time I did have when I wasn't goofing off on the computer. I wasn't mature enough back then to try and act like an adult all the time, but games created a level playing field. I tried to save most of the teenage angst for when I came home, much to my mother's dismay."

"The legendary Turner gaming addiction. Even while at college."

"It's bred true." He turned his face toward the sun and Tasha realigned a few of her early conceptions. He may have been advanced mentally, but he'd still dealt with the same stuff she had at that age.

"Still, it must have been tough."

Max shook his head. "I don't know that it was any tougher than being back in high school. It just was. I dealt with it. For the most part, I had a blast. And when I finished college, it was time to move on and be a grown-up, even if it didn't seem like I was old enough to most people."

Something suddenly stuck her. "When you asked me out that first time...?"

"Yup, I may have been seventeen, but I already thought you were more than simply a hot girl in a short skirt."

Tasha threw a pillow at him. "I didn't wear short skirts."

"Of course you did. There was this one especially that got me going. A Daisy Duke cut-off kind of thing. I nearly wore my cock out picturing you in it." Tasha sat speechless, her mouth

129

hanging open. "You're not planning on arguing with me, are you? Perfect recall, remember?"

She choked out an answer. "It's not that, it's the blunt sexual comments out of your mouth that tie me up in knots. I'm still trying to remember you're not off limits anymore."

He leaned forward and raked his gaze over her. Sexual intent flared, and suddenly the quiet evening of sharing was done and it was time to move to other more intimate matters. "Definitely not off limits. Are you done with your drink?"

She sipped slowly, to tease him. She'd discovered she enjoyed teasing him. "You're too efficient."

He put down his glass, stood and held out his hand. The heat in his eyes let her know exactly what he had planned. "I do my best."

And when their weekend was over, and they got back to reality to officially start their time together, it was soon clear that his best meant all-out concerted effort.

Chapter Twelve

The first morning she woke and didn't feel like getting out of bed, Tasha didn't say anything. It was too frightening to consider if she was pregnant, and too heart-wrenching if it turned out she wasn't.

Instead, she put it up to not being used to having a younger guy in bed with her. Confessing he could wear her out? The thought made her smirk—he certainly seemed to be trying hard enough, both in and out of the sack. Over the past month she'd lost five pounds from their newly established exercise program, not to mention all the sex. Combined with their decision to keep junk food out of the house, for the first time in four years she fit into her favorite designer jeans.

It was like having her own personal trainer twenty-four/seven.

Progress continued on her house construction, contrasting with a notable lack of progress when it came to mending fences with Lila. Her emails went unanswered, and she knew damn well Lila had to be screening her calls. The hurt inside ached at times. Tasha still hoped that whatever had gotten into Lila would smooth itself out, but until it did, there wasn't much more she could do.

She was surrounded by stubborn people. But at least when it came to Max, his ability to dig in his heels made sense, even when it drove her crazy. Ever since he'd moved in and they were forced into constant communication, there was no leeway given over things he thought were important. It made it tough to maintain emotional distance from the guy, because he always backed up his arguments with logic she couldn't deny.

While the physical attraction between them was clear, and man was she ever enjoying the attempting-to-get-pregnant part, she wanted more space. Not only because it had been over five years since she'd had a roommate of any kind. She needed some privacy, and soon, before the lines of friendship got even more blurred than they already were. Waking up to find herself cuddled up tight to him, or opening her eyes to discover him staring at her, gently stroking her hair back from her face—no way. No freaking way could she let that continue.

It was too dangerous. Screamed of all those other times she'd trusted someone with her heart and they'd turned around and taken advantage of her. Maybe Max would be different, but all she would acknowledge right now was his commitment to the idea of family. Not to her. Not yet.

She had to guard her heart. Time for desperate measures.

Tape measure in hand, she eyeballed the second bedroom of the apartment. It was crowded with her exercise bike and the tables Max had set up to put his computer equipment on. "You know, I think if we got one of those Murphy bed things we could fit it in here."

Max looked up from where he was working, confusion blurring his features for a second. "Are you expecting guests?"

"No, for you. Until we move into the house and you can have your own room. Here, give me a hand." She held one end of the tape toward him and slipped toward the corner to measure the space between the closet and the wall. "I mean, once I'm pregnant, we don't need to keep sharing a bed. We don't even need to share a bed now. Except for sex."

He nodded slowly as he took the other end of the measure and held it to where she pointed. "I see. Can I make a suggestion?"

He waited until she acknowledged him, then gave a sharp tug on the measuring tape. The end she held flew from between her fingers, slapping against his chest.

"Max, what the hell are you doing?"

He dodged around the computer chair and snagged her hands in his. He slowly wrapped the tape around both her wrists as he spoke, holding her firmly in spite of her wiggled attempts to escape. "My suggestion is—no. Moms and dads sleep together."

"But—"

"Get used to it. I'm not having a separate room from you so down the road we need to come up with all kinds of explanations for our kids."

"We could switch things up later." Oh God, he'd said kids. Like it was real and would be happening.

"Nope. May as well start now. That will give us a spare room in the house." He tugged her closer with her immobilized hands between them. "Does this mean that you were planning on giving up sex once you get pregnant? I don't remember that in the prenatal agreement."

Busted. "It's not, but—"

"Because I don't think either of us would enjoy that idea. If we're honest. I like having sex with you."

Max nuzzled her neck and she gave up. And gave in, refusing to think too hard about the warm feeling his stubborn response lit inside.

"You're such a pain in the ass," she grumbled.

"Of course if you start snoring—then all bets are off and we'll talk."

He grinned, untied her, and went back to his project.

That was another thing that amazed her—the way the man worked. He could have four things on the go at one time, and seem to keep them all moving forward simultaneously. Tasha shook her head and went back to her own work, carefully double-checking her blueprints and not attempting to imitate his seemingly chaotic approach. Anyone who pulled details together as randomly as he could made her suspicious.

A couple days later he was the one looking at her with suspicion as she sat up carefully and maneuvered her legs over the edge of the bed. A groan escaped, one hand rising to cover her mouth.

"So...?" He wandered around the end of the bed to stare down at her.

The rising nausea in her belly made her move slowly. "So, that casserole your cousins pawned off on us wasn't my favorite. I think it's repeating on me."

She stood and swayed. He grabbed on instantly, his strong arms supporting her as the room spun.

Concern wrinkled his brow. "I think the casserole was fine."

No, no, it definitely wasn't. Tasha pushed herself free and barely made it to the bathroom in time.

He helped, quietly soothing her even as he pulled her hair out of the way and tied it back with an elastic band. Gave her a cold facecloth and rubbed her back until the shakes passed. Handed her a glass of water to rinse her mouth out.

Then he handed her a pregnancy-test kit.

She swallowed around the horrible taste in her mouth, now half caused by nerves. After all her planning and plotting, he might have handed her a snake.

Her mind raced. What if it was positive? What if she'd managed to get pregnant? Suddenly this whole arrangement they'd pulled together would be permanent and she'd have to face that fact.

Or worse, what if she wasn't?

"It's too early to know."

Maxwell raised a brow. "I'm damn sure you are, from all the other signs, but humor me. These things are supposed to be able to pick up within a few days of conception."

Other signs? Was she stupid or did he really think he could spot this faster than she could? "Fine, but I'm not peeing with you in the room."

He rolled his eyes and dodged her feeble attempt to hit him, pulling her close and kissing her cheek in spite of her protests. "Hey, don't worry about it. If you're not pregnant yet, we'll keep trying. It's tough work, but I don't mind." He snatched up his toothbrush before backing away. He waggled his brows and she blew a raspberry at him.

"Did you at least buy the easiest test to figure out?"

He nodded. "If you'd like me to help you—"

"No. Thank you, but I'm not ready to share that pleasure, okay?"

Maxwell paused at the door. "Once you're done, give me a shout. I want to...be there, please?"

They stared at each other and a warmth rose inside that had nothing to do with being embarrassed and everything with appreciating how caring he'd been. She nodded, he left. It took a face wash in icy-cold water, followed by a thorough tooth brushing before she felt human enough to face the packaging. She opened the kit with shaking hands, followed the directions and laid the test stick on the counter.

Then she fled the bathroom.

Max stood in the living room, facing away from her, the muscles in his shoulders and lower back tight as he looked out the window. The early-morning sun shining into the room cast a homey glow over everything, and Tasha paused. They'd been enjoying each other's company the past weeks, getting to know one another better. She closed her eyes and fought to find that dividing line—she had to keep her emotional distance, no matter how great they got along. He'd never said a word about love; it had always been about choice and friendship. That's what she wanted, what she could rely on for the long run.

When people started tossing the *love* word around, that's when every one of her past relationships had broken down. She didn't want this to fall apart. It *couldn't* fall apart, not if that stick lying on the counter showed there was now a baby involved. Admitting they found a great deal of sexual pleasure in each other was fine, and friendship was fine. That's as far as she was willing to go.

She beat down the fluttering inside that questioned why she wouldn't want more. There was no way she would jinx this, not now.

Tasha went for as bright and happy an announcement as she could. Unfortunately, it came out sounding scared. "Set your timer, two minutes and counting."

Max enveloped her in a big hug. He rubbed her back in slow circles, and they stood there, waiting for the future to arrive.

"I don't think I can look," she confessed.

He hummed gently, soothing her. "I don't think you can not look. Again, I remind you we've got time. You're not *that* old."

She thumped him on the chest. "Not that old? You ass.

That's supposed to be reassuring?"

He smirked at her. "Well, I didn't think you'd like to hear statistics right now, but the fact is you're not old, and my age is in our favor, so..."

A short laugh escaped her. "I guess it's a good thing I grabbed a boy-toy then."

"Okay, now that's getting nasty."

She stuck out her tongue, and he hugged her again, and a whole minute passed. Standing still, her stomach gurgling lightly, his firm heartbeat under her ear, she felt like she was in a safe place, hiding away from all the potential dangers ahead. There was nothing she wanted more than that test to be positive. There was nothing she feared more. Everything would change. It was one thing to plan for a baby, another to have it actually happening. She clung to the tiny moment of calm, of not knowing for sure, while possibilities hovered, fraught with uncertainty.

Max tilted her chin up and kissed her. Soft, almost innocent. His toothpaste-tinged breath passed her cheek, and she closed her eyes and accepted his touch. Soaked in the distraction, accepted his caring, and marveled at how good a friend Maxwell had turned out to be.

It suddenly struck her how important this must be to him as well. All this time she'd been obsessing about having a baby, but it would be his child too. What was going through his head? Was he afraid, or worried about the future? Tasha wondered if there were expectations he had about being a father, things he'd learned from the Turner clan. Or if he wondered if the leap in responsibilities would be too much for him. She kissed him back harder, trying to reassure *him* that everything would be okay.

When they separated, leaning back to look into each other's

eyes, she didn't feel nearly as afraid.

"You ready?" he asked.

No. But she nodded and walked with him into the bathroom. And when she saw the lines on the test read positive, she tucked herself against his chest and let him hold her as she cried.

It took three months to pass that magical point when she no longer felt green every single moment. The fear of losing the baby slowly ebbed as the weeks passed, and she made it through another prenatal checkup. In fact, her energy picked up enough that when she rolled over in bed and caught Maxwell still snoozing beside her, a wicked thought romped through her brain hard enough it simply had to be acted on.

Tasha adjusted herself carefully to lie close to his side before pulling the blankets back to reveal his firm upper body. The delicate dusting of hair on his chest swirled neatly down to a single line disappearing under the dark navy fabric covering his groin. He'd been sleeping in nothing but boxers lately, in spite of the dropping temperatures. He claimed she put off more than enough heat for them both.

Yeah, especially when he was around. Except with all the throwing up and physical changes, she hadn't been that interested in sex lately. As in, they'd gone from daily to once a week if she could stay interested for that long. This morning a lack of interest didn't seem to be a problem. She stroked a single finger down his chest, dipping into his belly button, before tracing the edge of his elastic waistband while she considered how nice it was to have her libido back.

His cock twitched behind the loose fabric of the boxers. *Hmm.* Even though he wasn't awake, parts of him seemed to be registering her presence. She cupped him lightly and thrilled as his cock hardened, fast enough she knew the reaction was in response to her. The edge of his waistband was lower on one side than the other, bunched up by his hips, and as his cock expanded, there was a noticeable loss of room.

The rounded tip nudged past the top of the elastic to peek at her and she took a deep breath. Oh yes, this was getting very interesting indeed. She leaned over and breathed softly, letting her warm air wash over him.

His hips jerked.

Tasha found his responses fascinating, hooking a finger under the elastic and carefully pulling it down to reveal more of his length. She licked gently, then harder, before sucking the head of his cock into her mouth and swirling her tongue around the ridge.

"Sweet heaven on earth. I must have been a very, very good boy this year. If this is all I get for Christmas, I'm happy."

She pulled back with a slight *pop.* "You're easy to please."

"That I am." He propped himself up on his elbows and smiled down at her. "Don't let me interrupt you."

She paused for a second to grab her pillow and arranged it to help support her head, then she took hold of his hips and pulled him toward her, letting his erection slip smoothly back into her mouth. He rocked his hips slowly, not pushing too far, letting her concentrate more on sucking as he pulled back rather than trying to go in all the way. She played with his balls, rolling them in her fingers, and he groaned loudly, tracings of his seed escaping to paint her tongue with his flavor.

Tasha took pleasure in the sounds from his lips that floated down to her. She really had been fortunate when she hooked up with him. Max had been extremely supportive over the last while as she struggled to keep herself going through the tiredness and nausea. Their sex life had very much been put on hiatus, and yet he'd never complained.

Now was as good a time as any to make it up to him.

Max seemed to have other ideas, reaching down to smooth a strand of hair back from her cheek. He stroked her jaw gently, teasing the seam between her lips and his cock for a second before retreating completely, drawing his hips back.

She tilted her head to pout at him. "I was enjoying myself."

He pulled her up the bed and draped her on top of him. "I was enjoying myself too, but if you're feeling up to fooling around, I don't want your mouth."

With a gentle sway of his hips, he pressed his erection against her, and suddenly she couldn't wait to have him inside again. It had been too long, and she definitely had an eager partner.

Still... "Can I be lazy and make you do all the work?"

His eyes lit up and he rolled her slowly, supporting his full weight as they switched positions. "I do believe that's possible."

He rocked forward to kiss her forehead, then her nose. Dropped a quick kiss on her lips that she returned before he slipped his way down her body, stripping off her sleep shirt and panties and revealing her body to his heated gaze.

The physical changes so far were small, but she'd particularly felt an increase in her breast's sensitivity. The light touch of his forefinger as he drew gentle circles around her areolas was just the right amount of contact to tease her without causing pain. She held her breath as he put his mouth on one nipple, but the delicate dabbing of his tongue against her skin felt amazing, and desire grew between them.

His every touch was deliberate, so careful and precise. Tasha reveled in it and finally let go of her tension. Max played her body like she was a rare treasure, increasing her arousal without ever making her cringe from an oversensitized backlash. He licked and sucked, stroking her until she grew feverishly hot, the ache between her legs needing to be answered. When he pressed into her, the width of his girth seemed to have grown larger since the last time, and he had to rock in, small bits at a time as she pulled up a leg to try to accommodate him better. A wash of pleasure rolled over her, not only in her core, but her skin as he continued to stroke wherever he could reach—her breasts, her belly, the hard nub of her clit.

There was no wild thrusting, none of the harsh, almost animalistic pleasure they'd shared in the first days of their sexual relationship. Tasha watched Max's face as he joined them together, enjoying the play of emotion displayed there. The arousal, the tenderness. She couldn't have asked for a better friend in her life, in or out of her bed, and when the first pulses of her climax started, constricting around his shaft, she spoke his name, accepting his kiss as he too found release.

They lay tangled together for a while, his weight strategically resting to the side even as he left their bodies connected. It was very intimate, and very right.

Max rested a hand on her belly. There was no change yet, nothing to show they had a baby on the way. Tasha had given it a lot of thought, and even though she was now okay with them telling people, the first announcement wasn't going to be at the full out-and-out Turner-clan Christmas bash. No way would they share during that kind of insanity. Max had agreed—he suggested if they told his parents, Maxy, and his grandmother, the trickle-down effect of the big family network would be enough.

Tasha had already called her own mom and got a noncommittal "congrats", given with about the same degree of enthusiasm that Mom had used when she'd called to say she and Max were married. No, it was clear that her extended family was now the Turners. And all of them were being as supportive she'd hoped, except for one notable exception.

"You ready to head to the Turner Christmas dinner?" he asked.

Damn. She swore he was psychic at times. She sighed lightly, rolling to run her fingers through his hair in an attempt to calm her suddenly shaky nerves. "Honestly? Yes and no. The dessert is in the fridge, and that's all we have to bring, but I'm..."

The sentence didn't need to be finished. He knew what caused her hesitation.

Lila.

Chapter Thirteen

Max watched his wife wander through the family room in his Gramma's enormous home, chatting with everyone, older and younger.

His wife.

There was an immediate heart-wrenching, stomach-twisting response to that word every time he thought it, and he thought it often just to enjoy the sensation. Tasha was exactly what he'd longed for. Yeah, the past few weeks she'd spent a lot of days a pale shade of green, but his attraction to her was based on more than her natural beauty. Her sarcastic wit may have been a trifle slower in the mornings, but now that she'd reached her second trimester, the old spunk and devil-may-care attitude had snuck back into play, and he was even more in love than before.

Adding in the fact that was his baby growing in her belly? Over the moon. He could barely breathe every time the reality of it hit him.

The only taint in paradise was that she still had some kind of wall raised between them. At times she would laugh with him, cry with him. Whisper his name as they made love—and even thinking about sex with Tasha made his body tighten. But occasionally he caught her staring off into space with a sad expression, or in the middle of laughing with him she would almost physically pull back. Retreat. Straighten her shoulders and slide that damn wedge between them again. When he'd started this relationship he'd assumed that the details would fall into place—it was proving far more difficult than he'd imagined.

He obviously needed to increase the romancing again, but that had been difficult when her head was so often in the toilet.

"Hey, stranger."

Max twirled at his sister's call and hooted with delight. He grabbed her for a hug. "I've missed you."

She squeezed him back, even as she laughed lightly. "Yeah, yeah, I don't think missing me has been on the top of your things-to-think-about list lately."

Maxy backed away and waved as she looked over his shoulder. He pivoted in time to see Tasha respond and that shot to his gut went off again. "It has been busy, between the house and the—"

"Give me a break, I'm not complaining." She smirked at him. "I certainly hope when I'm a newlywed you don't expect me to be concentrating on too much outside of my immediate area. You guys are still on your honeymoon as far as I'm concerned. That excuses a lot of mental lapses and...*ahem*...skipped emails."

A streak of guilt ripped past him. "I was supposed to send you a few projects to proof. Shit, I can't believe I forgot."

She grinned. "Sorry, couldn't resist giving you grief. I'm serious—I don't expect you to be perfect right now, bro, but I do need a little guidance next week, or right after New Year's, if you don't mind. There's a section in that project you gave me where I'm fudging a step—and I can't untangle my coding errors, so it's not working."

"No trouble." But not during the holidays. Those romantic

memory-making things he wanted to put into place included a lot of private time for just him and Tasha. "At the start of January we'll get together and work it out."

A couple of the younger clan members darted underfoot and they both shifted their footing easily with the experience of years of attending crowded family events. "You two want to join me and Jamie after dinner for a walk?"

Max jerked upright. "You still seeing that guy?"

She grumbled back, "Yes, I'm still seeing him. We've been going out for the past three months." The front door opened and she peered hopefully in its direction. Max followed her gaze, but it was just kids running in and out from the porch to the main house.

"So, where is he now?" Max asked.

"He'll be here." Her cheeks flushed and he wondered what the hell was going on. Protective instincts kicked into high gear.

"Maxy, is something wrong?"

She shook her head rapidly. "Of course not. He's...not very punctual. It bugs me a little."

"Jerk. He's not pushing you anymore, is he?"

She flapped her fingers rapidly, motioning him to silence, then tugged him into a corner where they were no longer in the middle of the action. "Don't do that. It's bad enough you're giving me the third degree, I don't need everyone in the family asking what's up."

Max leaned back on the wall. His position let him see his sister, and still keep an eye on Tasha as she visited. "Sorry, you're right. But ever since that date when he pushed you too hard... I don't trust him, okay?"

Maxine fluffed her bangs, her fingers fidgeting. "He didn't push, only he wanted to go faster than I wanted to. It was no big deal."

Since it had interrupted his and Tasha's first sexual encounter, maybe the incident was etched harder on his brain than on hers. "So you're saying he's not doing that anymore?"

"He's not making me do anything I don't want to do, no."

And wasn't that a non-answer to his question. Before he could dig any deeper, the front door opened again and this time they both reacted. Not only had Jamie finally arrived, he'd shown up at the same time as Lila. Max couldn't let *that* situation go on any longer without intervention.

He gestured politely, motioning for Maxine to go ahead of him. "I guess we should go say hello to Twinkle Toes."

She slapped his arm. "Don't be a turkey."

They walked together toward the door. "Sorry, brotherly territorial rights and all that. Just..." He pulled her to a stop for a moment. "Be careful, okay? I don't think he's a bad guy, but I think you could do better."

She patted his cheek and went to grab a horrified Jamie away from the children circling his ankles. Max stopped himself from sniffing in disgust. Okay, that was it. He was moving Maxy and her pretty boy up the to-do list. Maybe a few choice questions over dinner would be enough to either scare the guy off or make him shape up, because right now? Max wasn't too impressed.

He turned to his cousin, offering his hand to take her coat. She was another one he wasn't too impressed with, but with her, at least, he had the ties of family. That gave him the right to let her know what he thought without any farting around.

"Afternoon, Junior." She turned to walk away, but that wasn't good enough.

"We need to talk."

Lila glared at him. "I don't know that we *need* to do anything, but since you asked so politely..."

She strode across the room to nearly the same spot he and Maxine had been standing, the tall floor-to-ceiling windows letting in the December sun and filling the area with a lot more warmth than came from his cousin and her sour expression. One deliberate crossing of her arms later and her body language screamed *shut up*. He laughed.

"Very nice, now how about you throw a bucket of cold water on me and announce to the room that I'm a blood-sucking lowlife. I doubt it will make you feel any better, but you'd get it out of your system."

"Don't be stupid, you haven't done anything wrong."

Max fought his temper. "But you've refused to speak with Tasha for almost three months, and you ignore her at family functions. You only answer the phone if I call or email."

"Right. See? I'm not mad at you."

Damn it all. "You're supposed to be older than me and more mature, stop acting like a pouty twelve-year-old."

Lila narrowed her eyes. "Yes, I am older than you, aren't I? Gee, like ten years or so. Maybe I'm a totally different generation than you, and I don't see things the same way."

He wasn't going to step into that trap. "Or maybe it's not the years but the lack of maturity after all, at least on your part. You're telling me this is all because I'm younger than Tasha? You've turned your back on years of friendship because I fell in love with her?"

"I'm sorry, but I simply can't see your relationship as anything other than a mistake."

Max held up a hand to stop her from turning away. "I don't understand why you won't at least talk about it. Whatever the specifics are of this..." he waved his hands in the air, feeling very ineffective, "...misunderstanding between you. Can't you get together for a drink and try to smooth it over?"

She shook her head. "This isn't your business, and it's not really something I want to talk about at a family event. I promise to stay on the other side of the room, and if you'll do the same, we'll have no problems. Now if you don't mind, I'd like to go say hello to everyone before I have to leave. I can't stay for dinner, so you won't have to choose your seating to avoid me."

She walked away, her body tight and awkward as she carried her tension with her. It made no sense to him, the depth of her anger, and yet that emotion was definitely there. Something harsh must be hurting his cousin that she could be this bitter, this quickly.

Enough. There was other family he wanted to celebrate with, others who had completely welcomed Tasha as a new member.

As always, there was nothing quiet or calm about the gathering. Max spent the next two hours moving from group to group, visiting with aunts and uncles, teasing his nephews. The whole time he kept an eye out for Tasha, enjoying seeing her smile, hearing her laugh. She winked at him across the room right before he got hauled into an impromptu game of jacks with his nine-year-old cousins and impressed them all with his skills.

When he finally managed to pull himself free and track down Tasha, he found her with a group of the toddlers. One sat in her lap, another draped over her shoulder as they peered at the picture book she held. The expressions on Tasha's face grew exaggerated as she changed her voice to match the wild monsters in the story, or the fairies coming to the rescue. The realization that she'd be doing this with their child in a few years' time choked his throat so tight he had to turn away and retreat to the kitchen for a glass of water to calm himself.

There was nothing he had wanted more than to have a future with Tasha, and that future seemed to be arriving as ordered, and he was the luckiest bastard around. Now if he could just get her to fall in love with him, things would be perfect.

She'd seen him approach. Even as she read the familiar story, Max's broad shoulders and distinctive walk had caught her eye. Just before he'd turned away, a moment of doubt struck—the worried expression that had crossed his face seemed out of place. He'd seen her with the children. Was it only hitting him now that this would be their life in a very short while? Full-time parenthood? She finished the book, kissed the top of the little one's head, and passed him back to one of the teenage girls gathered in the area who were in charge of the children until dinner.

She caught up with him as the announcement was made for everyone to make their way toward the table. He pulled her close as a stream of hollering children raced past them down the narrow hall, and the comfort and familiarity of his body felt so right.

They had only a few minutes as the chaos settled in the great room.

"Hey. What's up?" Tasha slipped her hand along his cheek, holding him for a minute

He kept her trapped against him, even though the hall emptied out, his hands resting on the top of her hips. "Let's see. I don't like my sister's boyfriend, there's turkey *and* ham for supper, but no sweet potatoes because two of the family got their names mixed up in the email, and you smell delicious."

His mouth brushed hers and she smiled even as she responded with a quick kiss of her own. But that wasn't enough of an answer. "You seem distracted."

He snorted. "You're in my arms. Distraction at its finest."

"That silver tongue is working well tonight, I see."

Max rumbled, a sexy sound deep in his throat that made a shiver thrill up her spine. "I can show you exactly how well my tongue is working later, if you're interested."

Oh yes, now she was the one getting distracted. Max slipped his fingers through hers, drawing her to his side for a second and kissing her neck before leading her to a chair. As the rattling of plates and noise carried through the meal, he kept one hand constantly touching her.

Whatever had made him run and hide, she wasn't going to ask. Tasha took in all the smiling faces down the long length of the table and gave thanks she was able to be a part of the family.

Chapter Fourteen

Max brought Tasha back to Gramma's house a couple days after the big family gathering so they could tell her their news in private. Her enthusiastic response was exactly what he'd expected, and seeing the flush of delight on Tasha's face made it even better.

Unfortunately, his timing was bad, and they barely had a chance for a cup of tea before the visit was cut short. Gramma kissed him and Tasha, then took hold of Uncle Maxdean's arm, using him to help negotiate her way down the wide front steps. She spoke as she walked, her voice clear and strong as always. "Now I want you both to come back another day when I don't have to run off. Tasha, I'll be sure to find those albums I promised. And don't you fuss about looking around the place without me here. Make yourself at home."

"Love you, Gramma," Max called after her.

"I know, but it bears repeating," she called back and he laughed, leaning on the doorframe. Their standard response, filled with the familiarity of love.

When he turned, Tasha stood beside him, contentment etched on her face. "She's amazing. I've always loved visiting with her, and to think I'm now related to that wonderful woman makes me warm, no matter how cold it is outside."

Max shut the door before pulling her against him. He

couldn't seem to get enough of touching her. Holding her close. "You made her very happy yourself just now, telling her about having another great-grandchild on the way."

"She did seem pleased."

"Pleased? I thought she was going to get up and dance a jig, she was so excited."

Tasha smoothed his hair, running her fingers along his nape and his motor revved. She definitely seemed to be over the bump in terms of not wanting to be touched. It was making his plans for romancing her and trying to build a stronger connection between them both easier and harder. Easier, because she was willing to spent lots of intimate time with him. Harder—well, there had to be more to their relationship than sex, but that was difficult to explain to his body.

Her face lit with excitement. "You ready to show me around? That was sweet of her to offer to let me take a peek around when she found out I've never really had a chance to explore the house. Especially since she already had an appointment."

"I honestly had no idea she had other plans today, or I would have arranged our visit for another time."

Tasha pulled him toward the stairs, her fingers threaded through his. "That was a long-enough visit. We just had Christmas dinner two days ago, and you know there will be a ton of other family events over the next weeks."

Then Tasha got lost in architectural design, admiring the construction and details of the old family home. He followed her from room to room, loving the exclamations of delight that escaped as she found some new feature that she'd studied about but never actually seen before. They went through every room in the house on the first and third floors. They skipped the rooms that his grandmother still used on the second floor—

the master bedroom, and a couple others that contained her personal effects.

Three hours later he still had a grin on his face. Tasha's enthusiasm flowed out of her in a constant stream as she shared ideas for slight modifications to their house under construction. He tugged her into the kitchen and pressed her onto one of the tall stools before handing her a glass of juice. She sipped without thinking, then blinked in surprise. "Oh, that is good. My mouth was so dry."

Max grinned. "That's what happens when you talk for hours straight."

She glanced at her watch. "No. Way."

"Way. I didn't think you had it in you, to be that kind of chatterbox. Well, except when you're very tipsy." He stepped around to rub her shoulders, the tight muscles relaxing under his hands as she leaned back into him.

"Don't nag about that. But you should have said something when I lost track of time. I didn't mean to waste your afternoon."

He slid his thumbs along the tendons in her neck and she moaned. His body tightened at the sound. "It wasn't a waste at all. I told you, this entire week is a holiday for me, and I want to spend it with you."

The height of the stool forced her to look up at him as she twisted to face him, her cheerful face a pleasure to witness. When she wrapped her arms around his waist, his body nestled between her open thighs. It was comfortable and easy and her smile was real.

Then that damn shadow intruded again. He swore he saw it—as if a physical cloud actually rolled between them. She shifted her position, lowering her hands to rest on his hips, pressing her body away from him slightly.

153

"That's sweet of you. I enjoyed your company. I guess we should head home soon."

What the hell? All the ease of her flowing conversation of the past hours disappeared into awkward phrases that were completely unlike her. Tasha stood, brushed past him and moved toward the door.

"What's wrong?" He hurried after her, worried about both her and the baby.

Tasha shook her head. "Nothing. Should we go?"

"Are you sure? Do you feel okay?"

"I'm fine. But we should go."

Max scrambled for inspiration. Whatever weird thing had just happened, he wasn't going to let it disrupt the good memories of this day. "I wanted to show you something."

She checked her watch again. "You're sure you don't have anything you need to do?"

He forced himself to laugh as naturally as he could, even as his mind raced to figure out what was wrong. "Tasha, I'd swear you were trying to get rid of me or something. Come on, I have nowhere to be, and neither do you. Indulge me. Please?"

She accepted his hand, and he led her back onto the porch, walking slowly along the wide covered veranda that wrapped around the entire house. He kept their hands together, rubbing his thumb lightly over the back of her knuckles. To their left, the surface of the small pond rippled with tiny waves, the slight wind disturbing the surface. The trees swayed, and when she shivered, he pulled her under his arm. Around the first corner the wind died away, blocked by the house, and he pointed to the massive porch swing. "Our destination."

The firm cushion on the oversized bench seat sank only a little as they arranged themselves. Tasha sat primly at his side, her hands lying in her lap as she gazed at the land surrounding his grandmother's home.

He rested his arm along the top of the bench seat, drawing circles on her shoulder lazily as he got the swing rocking. Max kept silent, spinning through their conversation in his mind, everything they'd done since arriving at the house, but he couldn't think of a single thing that would have made her turn formal all of a sudden.

Screw it. He nuzzled under her ear, kissing her neck. If she wanted to be stiff, he'd find a way to relax her. Tasha arched her neck, opening up to his touch, and he smiled against her skin. Even if there was something going on in her brain he didn't understand, he had learned enough to push her hot buttons. Her remaining tense wasn't going to make her any more open to confessing what was on her mind. Keeping the swing moving with a gentle motion, he twisted to face her, leaning across her body to slip his fingers into her hair and cup her neck.

He kissed her gently, smoothing his lips over hers, playing with his tongue over the seam of her mouth. She let out a sigh and he felt her loosen up as she kicked off her shoes and snuggled against his side.

All the while, he kissed her, stroking his tongue into her mouth, nibbling on her lips. She moved closer, pressing him back against the bench and straddling his thighs, her hands cupping his face, her body swaying sensuously over his. Oh yes, that was much better. Whatever she was worried about had been pushed aside. Hopefully forgotten. A breeze floated past and she shivered, tucking herself tightly to him.

There were only the light noises of nature on the air, and the wet sounds of their kisses, the heavy intake of breathing as their excitement revved up a notch. He slipped his hands between their torsos to undo her buttons, rearranging her breasts by folding the tops of her bra in half and creating a shelf for the heavy globes to rest on. Then he lifted her to a more upright position, bringing his mouth in line with his goal.

The swing rocked and she jerked, catching her balance.

"Grab my shoulders. I won't let you fall." He held her hips and covered one breast with his mouth. Immediately after lowering her hands to his shoulders, she dug in her nails. Her back arched, giving him greater access to every inch of skin as he laved in long, slow strokes around the sensitive peaks.

He deliberately planted his feet on the ground and swung the bench forward, forcing her toward him, then he swayed in the other direction, holding firmly to her hips but causing her upper body to retreat slightly. She laughed, joy and happiness back in her voice, and his heart lightened. That's what he needed, what he wanted. To have Tasha be herself—the woman he'd fallen in love with. The one who loved life and greeted every day with enthusiasm.

Side to side he alternated on every rock until she squirmed.

"More, I need more."

She ground her hips down, the heat of her sex passing through the layers of material between them and making him crazy.

"You trust me?"

She looked him straight in the eye as he held his breath. "Of course."

"I'm pretty sure this will work, but let's check." He cupped under her hips, and rose. She clung to him, her arms wrapping around his neck.

Her lips distracted him again, and he stopped to kiss her for a moment, letting her slip down his body until she stood crowded against him, feverish heat rising between them to counter the slight chill in the December air. Here on the backside of the house, there were no neighbors to be seen. The house faced the pond and the distant trees on the back of the acreage. He eyed the levels carefully. Oh yeah, it should work.

"Kneel on the bench."

Tasha grabbed the side support with one hand and laughed. "What are you up to?"

"You'll see soon enough." He stepped closer, sliding his hands around her waist, until he reached her buttons and zipper. Undoing her pants only took a moment, then he wiggled them past her hips to leave her naked ass facing him.

"You're insane, Maxwell."

Down on his knees behind her, he pressed his cheek against her bare butt and licked. "Not insane. Creative. Hold on tight."

He had other things in mind, but this had to be explored. With his knee wedged under the swing to brace it in place, and one hand still wrapped around her hips, he trailed the fingers of his other hand up the naked skin of her inner thigh until he touched the entrance to her sex.

She shuddered. "This is crazy."

"Yup. Open your legs wider."

Tasha obeyed, then let out a squeal as he bent her toward him, exposing her to his mouth. She was wet, and as he explored with his tongue, she blessed his ears with a steady stream of moans and squeals and breathless mutterings until he couldn't wait another minute.

"Get a good grip on the back of the bench and press your hips toward me." Max waited until she'd gotten into position before hauling the footstool over. He admired the shape of her ass as he opened his jeans and released his aching cock. "I've always loved the view from the swing, but this is better than I remembered."

Tasha glanced over her shoulder and shook her head. "Screw the jokes. You need to hurry up."

He adjusted the footstool until it was directly below the swing, knelt on it and lined his cock up. It took one slow pass to bury his shaft entirely in her warm welcoming body.

Oh my word. Tasha let out a low cry of approval as he filled her, dropping her head to rest on her hands where she clung to the bench. "Okay, insane or not, this feels great."

She squeezed him and Max reacted. His fingers where he gripped her hips dug in deeper, and she relished the sensation. This was what she needed. Something raw and wild to take her mind off the doubts that insisted on tormenting her when she least expected them. For just a little while, she didn't want to ponder if her relationship with Maxwell was going to last. Didn't want to imagine what she'd do if he didn't keep his promise and she were suddenly left on her own.

Didn't want to think about how afraid she was that she might be falling in love with him.

So she pressed back on him harder, looking for the physical connection to distract both of them for a while.

He applied pressure to her hips, the motion carrying down to push the swing away easily, his erection retreating from her body and suddenly she figured it out. "You're kidding me. This is pretty kinky stuff. You used this swing before?"

"Nope. Never like this, but damn, it looks like it's going to work." He released the pressure on her hips and the weight of the swing took her toward him, stabbing his rigid length deep at exactly the right speed.

"Oh God, yeah, it works." She closed her eyes and tried to ignore the fact her pants were bunched around her knees, and that he was still fully dressed except for his cock hanging out, now hidden from sight in her body. "Please tell me people don't regularly go trespassing on Gramma Turner's land. I don't need anyone seeing this."

His hand slid over the rounds of her ass as he continued the steady rocking back and forth. "No one can see but me. And I see everything. Your lips cling to my cock then open—" He choked to a stop.

A wave of arousal slid over her as the tightness in his voice sent her higher. The cut-off words, his evident lust—registered deep. He couldn't even speak, and his shaft seemed to expand, growing even harder and hotter within her body. He picked up the pace, not simply allowing the bench to swing, but using momentum to make each slam of her ass against his groin that much firmer. She wasn't frightened the motion was too rough with the rest of her body so well supported.

Her breasts swayed, hanging below the bra he'd moved aside. The edge of the fabric teased her nipples on each rock, enough of a touch that tingles of pleasure threaded through her and boosted the impending climax building in her core.

Max drew the swing to a stop, wrapping an arm around her and pulling her upright against his chest. The folds of her blouse fell open, her breasts bare to his touch and he cupped one, his thumb lightly teasing her nipple against the side of his forefinger. He snuck a hand over her belly and between her legs, fingers unerringly reaching her clit. Somehow he found the leverage to continue to thrust upward, pressing into her with short stabs. All of the sensations combined together, the sensual touches, his heated breath. The sounds from the wind in the trees, that fact it was so wicked and risky to be making love out on the porch. Her orgasm took her by surprise and her

159

core pulsed around him. Max swore as he slowed, then froze deep inside before exploding.

He held her tight for a moment, then somehow got them both vertical and twisted around so she ended up sitting on his lap, still connected. Completely relaxed from her climax, she let him do the arranging of their limbs as he placed her pant-bound legs over his. He pulled her torso back until her head rested on his shoulder and his warm hands languidly roamed over all the bare skin he could reach.

"That's about the dirtiest thing I've ever done." Tasha twisted her head slightly to rub her lips against his stubble-roughened cheek. He caught her lips with his and they kissed lazily, warm breaths combining as they relaxed.

He buttoned her shirt up without taking his lips from hers. She opened her eyes, but his face was still relaxed, eyes closed even as he dressed her. His cock slipped from her body and he helped her up, straightening and tucking himself away only after he'd made sure she was comfortable and covered. They held hands as they went back to shut up the house, then hit the road to return home. All the while the tenderness in his touch landed in layers and soaked into her soul.

Maybe this whole crazy thing wasn't a mistake. Maybe she could be brave enough to let go of a few more fears and learn to trust completely.

Chapter Fifteen

The muted sounds of medical equipment carried through the air, the clean scent of antiseptic and that not-quite-pleasant aroma of completely sterile surroundings. Max held on to Tasha fingers and tried not to squeeze too tightly.

"I'm dying here." Tasha wiggled uncomfortably on the bed, her softly rounded belly poking up under the pale blue of her maternity top. He reached with his free hand and stroked the place where their baby was growing. Six months, and there was no denying to anyone that another Turner was on the way.

"I offered to drink the water for you, but they said that wouldn't work very well." He brought his chair closer to the bed without having to let go with either hand, and she chuckled lightly, cutting off with a moan.

"Don't make me laugh or I'm going to pee right here on the bed. I think someone miscalculated how much liquid I needed to drink for this ultrasound to work. Oh..."

His heart leapt. "I felt that. The baby kicked." He palmed her belly gently, rubbing in slow circles. The sensation didn't get old—he'd been lying in bed for the past three weeks with his arm wrapped around Tasha, carefully holding her belly to catch as many of the increasingly noticeable movements as possible.

"This little tyke is getting more accurate in targeting vital spots. I know my bladder is full right now, but that doesn't make it open season." She dropped her head back on the pillow with a groan and Max's heart swelled with love. She'd been better lately about not cutting herself off from him emotionally, but there was still something missing. Some part she held in reserve, and that damn prenatal agreement bound his tongue. It was killing him not to blurt out how much she meant to him.

Especially at a time like this. A truly momentous occasion, a memory they would share forever.

He leaned closer and kissed her cheek, nuzzling against her as they waited for the clinician to join them. The faint scent of her soap filled his head, the smell of her skin connecting him with so many memories from the past months. He loved waking in the morning with her cuddled next to him, usually with one leg thrown over his like she was trying to make sure he couldn't run away.

She didn't need to worry. He wasn't planning on going anywhere.

Fluttering rumbles continued under his hand as their baby moved and his chest tightened. He had to get his mind on other things, or he was going to be bawling like a baby himself before too long. He brushed one final kiss against her temple before leaning back in his chair, reluctantly pulling his hand away.

"Did you arrange to take the rest of the day off?"

She nodded. "We need to stop in at the house sometime in the next while and make a few decisions about tile and taps and all sorts of things—the finishers have kept a list for us."

Max groaned. He'd always prided himself on being a good multitasker, but over the past weeks as he'd strived to be there for Tasha, the ability to juggle as many balls as usual seemed to elude him.

Somehow he'd find the time to get it all done, without her thinking he was neglecting her. All the advances he'd made in terms of having her open up to him, having her start to confide in him as more than simply a friend, gave him hope she was falling for him. Now if she'd stop being so damn stubborn and admit it, they could get somewhere.

They chatted quietly as she squirmed until there was finally a knock at the door and a gowned attendant joined them.

"Sorry for the wait, we'll be ready to roll in a jiffy." The woman held out a hand to Tasha. "I'm Nancy. You eager to get a peek at that little one?"

Tasha's face lit up. "You have no idea."

Nancy laughed. "Well, I'm sure when I push on your bladder you'll be debating how much you want these pictures, but yes, it's exciting." She turned toward him and smiled. "How nice. You brought your brother with you."

He couldn't stop his burst of laughter. "Husband. I'm the father of the baby you're taking pictures of in a minute."

The woman floundered for words, stammering out an embarrassed apology as she reached to grab plastic bottles from a warming tray. Max exchanged glances with Tasha. Her cheeks were flushed, but she rolled her eyes for a second then blew him a kiss. The difference in their ages had bothered very few people. Sure, there was the occasional question or a mistake like just now, but for the most part the only person who had made it into a huge issue was Lila.

Her continued avoidance of Tasha was more than rude, it was cruel. He checked Tasha again, hoping her thoughts hadn't drifted in the same direction as his. He didn't want the memory of Lila's stubborn betrayal of their friendship to have any part in this day.

Tasha focused on the clinician as she settled in her chair and rearranged Tasha's top to access her belly. Max rolled his chair closer, watching with fascination. Nancy was great, and explained each step as she proceeded. Tasha cringed when the monitor touched her skin, and he found his fingers and hers linked together again. He held her hand, silently enthralled as images appeared on the screen. Black and white blurs sharpened into focus, and suddenly there were tiny hands and feet. A little rounded bottom. Perfectly formed miniature shoulders.

Happiness struck him like the broadside of a wave. It threatened to crash him to his knees, his blood pounding in his ears so hard he barely heard the rest of the explanations.

"Do you want to know what sex your baby is?" Nancy asked.

Max motioned for Tasha to answer. He'd already told her what he wanted, but it was up to her to decide.

She licked her lips, turning back to the monitor eagerly. "If you can tell us, we'd love to know."

Max leaned forward. *Yes.* He'd hoped to hear. Okay, maybe he had a touch of OCD, but it would make things a lot easier for planning, especially prepping the baby's room and...

He just wanted to know.

"All right, we'll take a look. There's a slight chance we won't be able to figure it out, and please remember there's a possibility we might be wrong."

The sound of his breathing echoed loudly in his ears as he waited.

Nancy clicked her tongue and made complaining noises. "Little one, stop rolling away from me. Looks like someone's pretty active right now."

Tasha was the one who put his fingers in a death grip. "I don't mind."

"Hmmm, I think if we try from this angle..." Nancy reached

around to the far side of Tasha's belly, angling the sensor back, and wonder of wonders, the baby stretched. "Oh, there we go. I do believe I don't see anything."

Max couldn't care less. Fine, he could paint the walls yellow and they'd come up with two sets of names. It didn't matter not knowing—

"Which usually means you're having a girl."

The room spun.

On the monitor, their baby—*his baby girl*—rolled again, presenting her feet toward the monitor and losing the focus. To his left, Tasha made a cooing sound, something halfway between a cry and a sigh.

He held it together by a thread until Nancy had wiped the gel from Tasha's belly, congratulated them both and left them alone. He barely managed to help Tasha to a sitting position before burying his face in her neck and letting the tears fall.

Tasha ached as Max wept, his arms cradling her tenderly. That something inside that longed for a love without end—that place she'd had tied up tight and hidden away fearing it could never, ever be—snapped wide open.

She'd been thrilled to see the baby. Every step of the journey made this experience more incredible, and more real to her, but right now it wasn't just the joy of having seen her little girl that moved her.

Maxwell was tearing her heart in two.

It was the obvious love Maxwell had to share that made her tangle her fingers in his hair and hold him tight. She wished she could tell him she understood how he felt. That she had the same reaction when she saw him looking at *her* across the room with a smile on his face. She wished she knew the right words to use at this moment.

She wished she didn't need to pee so bad.

Tasha tugged lightly to get him to back up enough she could kiss his cheek, tasting the salty moisture of his tears. "It's okay. And I want to talk with you, but I've got to go to the bathroom or I'm going to have a terrible accident right here."

Max shook with his laughter as he escorted her down the hall, leaving her with a pat on the backside. Tasha shut the door on his grinning face, torn between needing to share with him, and the feeling she was literally about to explode.

She washed up quickly, stepping with relief into the waiting room. He stood from where he'd been leaning on the wall, took her hand and they made their way back down to the car in silence. His hand was warm around hers, gentle. Someone stepped in their path and instantly he was there, guarding her from being bumped on the busy sidewalk.

He was always doing that, she realized. Coming forward to protect her. Making light-hearted jokes when someone spoke out of line regarding their ages, or her being pregnant so fast. Without making a big deal of it, he'd been acting like a knight and holding a shield before her to keep things running as smoothly as possible.

The smile he gave her as he helped her into the car— sincere as always, but with an added twist of mischief in it. That was what she'd always appreciated about him before they'd gotten involved. The way he seemed to thumb his nose at the world around him even while showing what was important to him.

There was no denying this baby was important to him. He'd said she was important as well. She grabbed for his hand and clutched it the whole way home, not willing to talk, still searching for what to say.

Searching for the strength to acknowledge love had snuck in.

Tasha waited until they were back in their apartment before she pulled him to the bedroom. She made him sit, then crawled on top of him to shower him with mad kisses.

He cupped her face in his hands, slowing her down. Taking the time to answer her with long, wet kisses that turned the racing beat in her nerves into a racing pulse in her core. Then he dropped his forehead against hers and spoke quietly, and her heart overflowed.

"Oh my God, Tasha, that was the most incredible moment of my life, seeing our little girl." His hands swept down to cradle her belly and his body shuddered as he took in a deep breath. "I know it doesn't make any sense to some people, but I've truly wanted this forever. I've wanted to have a family of my own, with children and a lover to share my life.

"When we arranged this, with that prenatal agreement, I told you I'd always be there for this baby. I said this relationship between us was a choice. That's still true. It was, and I think being together is the best thing possible for us both. But I have to tell you something. When I agreed to this situation, I didn't tell you everything."

One finger lifted her chin until their eyes met. He stared at her, his pupils dark with the depth of his emotion. "I love you."

She held back her tears. Every word he spoke rushed in and chipped away another piece of the wall she'd built around her heart. Tasha lifted her fingers to his mouth.

He kissed them softly before continuing, his voice growing stronger as he spoke. "I know you said you didn't love me and that's okay, but I can't hide this anymore. I'm going to care for you with everything I've got and that means telling you the truth."

My God. Her throat tightened. Involuntarily, her old self-defense mechanisms kicked in. "You're in love with the baby, with the idea of family—"

"This isn't just about the baby, although I do love her. Holy *fuck*, we're having a girl..." His voice broke and she laughed through the tears falling from her own eyes.

"You need to stop swearing before that little girl arrives."

He nodded, his lips pressed together. He kissed her again, tilting his head to briefly catch her mouth with his. "I love you. I do. Nothing's going to change that. If you still need time, that's fine. But I've got to stop hiding how I feel. I don't expect anything from you except to give me a chance to prove it."

Fear that now he'd actually said the words he'd lose the feeling rocked her. She beat it down, refusing to let her apprehension immobilize her like it had before. This wasn't about her past, it was about her future. She had to move forward.

Be honest. Be upfront.

"I'm scared."

He frowned. "Of what?"

"That you'll leave me. That now you've admitted you love me, I'll do something wrong and you'll decide it's not worth the time and the energy. That I'm not worth it."

"Oh God, Tasha." He slipped one hand up around the back of her neck and cradled her tighter against him, the roundness of her belly pressing his torso. He rocked her like a baby, squeezing her close and for the first time she could remember, she let the tears fall. For the relationships that had gone sour. For the family who had turned their back on her. She'd stood on her own for so long that there was never an appropriate time for her to weep and mourn for what she didn't have in her life. She'd pushed aside the hurt and gone forward.

Only now she saw she'd simply been dragging the pain behind her.

She clung to him for the longest time, and he held her, letting her cry it out until there was nothing left to cry. Hiccups hit, and then the giggles as he soothed her. He rubbed her back, offered her tissues, walked her to the washroom and wet down a facecloth and wiped her eyes.

She grabbed a cloth and soaked it, tugging him closer and washing his face as well. With every touch she tried to show how much it meant to be able to trust him. How much she needed to have this become more than how they'd started.

When she finally felt human again, they ended up back on the bed, fingers tangled together as they lay side by side.

Letting go of the hurt brought both relief and regret. She didn't want to make this a day filled with bitter memories, but it seemed the emotional dam had burst and there was no way to stop the flood. She picked her pains carefully, trying not to lay blame, but to explain why her fears haunted her.

She stared into his eyes as she forced herself to speak. Watching his response—she wasn't sure it helped or made it more difficult to see his expression change as she shared.

"Every single time I've realized I loved a person, something has happened. The situation would change, and suddenly they would be gone. Or they would expect me to change, and when I didn't meet their expectations, it would be my fault, and the end result would be the same—I would be alone again."

He touched her cheek tenderly. "You're not responsible for other's actions."

She sniffed. "I know it in my head, but convincing my heart is a whole lot harder. I've read a million self-help books about how my father leaving my mother had nothing to do with me, but it still hurts."

Max nodded slowly. "And now you're worried I'll fall out of love with you? Is that why you've been running hot and cold on me? One minute you enjoy my attention, the next you put up barriers?"

Tasha breathed in slowly, fighting to stop the air from stuttering en route into her lungs. "Again, my brain trusts you, but I'm still scared. What if I don't get back my body after the baby arrives—will you still want to be with me? What if I'm too tired taking care of the little one to be interested in sex? I can't imagine you ever turning to another, you're not the type to cheat, but—"

The words stuck in her throat. Picturing Max in the arms of another woman was enough to make her sick to her stomach.

"Shh. Don't do that to yourself." He pulled her against his chest, his chin resting on top of her head. The warmth of his body wrapped around her, the tenderness in his words cradled her heart. "I love you. I love *you*, not someone you think you need to be for me. I can't erase your fears. I wish to God I could."

Tasha talked on. Just long enough for her to share a few more of the things she'd held in tight. It wasn't like Max offered any instant fix. He didn't have any magical words to share that washed away the past. But he listened, and the expression on his face said he cared. Cared deeply. His few words were comforting, loving. Exactly what she needed to hear.

When she'd let the last drop escape, they both lay quietly for a while. A tranquil peacefulness surrounded them, like the calm after the storm. He pulled one hand free and smoothed her hair back. "Are you going to be okay?"

She nodded quickly, not wanting the tears to return before she had a chance to finish. It took three tries and a couple throat clearings to be able to force the words out.

"You know that prenatal agreement? Can I change my mind about one detail?"

He teased lightly. "You want to add something about me groveling at your feet on a daily basis?"

She hit him, then returned his smile. "Max, I'm still scared, but I'd..." A deep breath in to steady her nerves. This was what she wanted. It was what she needed. "I'd like to let myself fall in love with you."

A sparkle of amusement flashed in his eyes. "That sounds like work."

Damn. "I didn't mean it that way."

He laughed as he slid his hand down her body until it rested on her belly. He didn't look away from her, keeping her captivated by the longing reflected in his face. "I want you to trust me. I want you to love me."

"It's hard. To let go of the past."

Max nodded slowly, his hand massaging in gentle circles over her belly. His words came quietly. "This baby has done nothing, and yet I love her. Try to remember that."

She nodded. He kissed her and made as if to sit up. Tasha gripped him by the T-shirt. This wasn't how she wanted this to end, this whole emotional rollercoaster. It needed one thing to come to completion.

She pulled him back to the bed and made love to him.

Softly. Slowly. Getting him to help when she asked, but taking the reins as often as she could. He stripped off his shirt when she tugged it free of his pants. Once she'd undone his zipper and pressed the top of his pants open, he wiggled out of them, turning to help remove her clothing. Tongues touched, dancing together as they kissed. The salty tang of tears blended together with the passion rising between them as she stroked his shaft in one hand, the fingers of her other hand locked in the hair at the back of his neck. She nibbled on his lips, kissed her way down his neck. Licked his nipples and the muscles crossing his abdomen. When she laved the broad head of his erection, he shuddered, his hands skipping momentarily from where they'd been floating lazily over her skin.

Tasha covered him with her mouth and pressed down, getting him wet, holding the rest of his length in her fist as she moved over him. She wanted to give to him, care for him like he'd been caring for her. It was a lame attempt, because no matter how good it might feel physically, there was no way she could possibly match what had built inside her emotionally.

He pulled her off far sooner than she wanted, arranging her over his thighs.

"I need you," he whispered.

The room hushed around them—no music, no sounds of nature. Just them, and their breathing and, as she lifted her hips and reached down to try to guide him into her body, their laughter.

"I can't reach," she admitted sheepishly. Her belly wasn't that big, but the angle was enough to hinder her attempt.

Maxwell sat up and adjusted himself, the wet head of his cock slipping between her folds so smoothly. She took him deep and sat still, savoring the moment. Her hands rested on his shoulders, her fingers playing over the firm muscles.

He lifted her head, and there was a light in his eyes—blinding. Brilliant. Full of joy and something else. He spoke against her lips.

"This is part of love."

Pleasure danced as he lifted and lowered her hips carefully. Each time his erection pierced her body it sent new sensations singing through her, and all the while he whispered to her. Soft love words. He told her they were all the things he'd been saving up over the past months. All the things he'd been longing to tell her. Her heart expanded to the point she would soon have no room to draw a breath. And when they reached a climax together, there was a moment she swore she heard all three of their heartbeats.

Chapter Sixteen

Tasha's stomach was going to ache for the rest of the day from laughing so hard.

"And then there was the time—"

Tasha held up a hand in an attempt to restrain her sister-in-law's enthusiasm. "Maxy, you've got to stop. Your brother is going to kill you for giving me all this dirt on him."

Maxine waved a hand and took a sip of her coffee. "He knew it was going to come out eventually. You need the background when you want to tease him down the road. Or tease your kids about how much like their father they are."

Her heart thumped out a rapid beat at the thought of a whole family with Maxwell. She hid her smile in her teacup. The demons of doubt were still there, rattling at her mind, but she'd promised herself to try to trust. Try to maintain a positive attitude toward their relationship, and so far, it was working. Still, it had only been a few days—it wasn't going to be easy to put aside years of apprehension so quickly.

She glanced up at Maxwell's sister, grinning at the shining expression on her face. It was much easier to remain positive when she was around someone like Maxy, who seemed to take on everything with a wholehearted blur of excitement. All that shared energy had to be either invigorating or positively nauseating.

Today, Tasha was going for the energizing side of the equation.

"Tasha, can I ask you something?"

"Of course." She leaned back in the chair, and a strange sense of déjà vu stole over her. They were back at the Sugar Shack—the same shop where Maxwell had first proposed to her. With her belly swelling before her, she felt a whole lot better this time round than the last.

"When did you move out on your own?" Maxine asked.

Tasha thought about it for a minute. "I left for college and never moved back."

"Like Junior."

She shook her head. "I didn't really have a place to go home to, so I had to leave. Your brother chose to move out."

Maxy sighed. "And I chose to stay home. When I did move out last year, I moved in with my friend Valerie." The bright shining smile faded as Maxine wrinkled her nose.

"What's wrong with that?"

"Nothing terrible. I just think I'd like to be completely on my own for a while, but I don't know that it's the right thing to do."

Ahhh, it began to make sense. "Since you're never on your own now?"

Maxy's wry expression combined with her nodding acknowledgement. "Bingo. I love my family, but if you've noticed? The Turner clan can be overwhelming at times."

There was no holding in her laughter. "Um, I noticed. But why not move out? I mean, you'd have to find a place you can afford, but if you're not too fussy, you can do it. You should have seen my first apartments. Tiny things, but they were my own."

Maxy waggled her head. "I know it makes sense, in a way, but right now Valerie needs a roommate, and there's no real reason to move out." She shrugged. "It's something that's been going through my mind, I guess. I'll think about it a bit more." Maxy popped straight up in her chair, all her concern shedding off like droplets from a raincoat. "What are you up to for the rest of the day?"

Oh, to have her sister-in-law's energy. "I have two final projects to complete. Once they're done I'm off indefinitely— which will give me time to have this baby and hopefully get my brain back before I have to jump back into the work fray. Not to mention getting the house done. Max and I are meeting there this afternoon."

"It's nearly finished, right?"

"Getting closer." Thank God. She'd never have dreamed that the house building would take longer than the baby building. "I'm used to drawing up the plans and that's the end of it. Since I took on the contracting to save money, the delay's partly my fault. The latest estimate is a month to completion. There's still no flooring down—and the guys laying the tile are running behind—and until that happens, it won't feel real."

"It's going to be beautiful when it's done, though."

Tasha smiled. "I'm looking forward to being able to move in. What are you up to?"

"I'm heading over to the house to have lunch with Gramma. Do you want to get together later this week? I can help you with the secret room."

"Shhh." Tasha held up a finger to her lips. "Not a word about that. I don't want Max to find out before I'm ready to tell him. I'm still figuring things out."

Maxy leaned back in her chair and pretended to pout. "Fine. Then I'll help with the baby's room. I saw the most adorable set of curtains the other day. Oh, and I found a bib with *Samantha* on it, and I bought it for you."

Tasha laughed softly as she reached to squeeze her hand. "You're going to be the best auntie ever, you know that?"

Maxy grinned. "That's the plan. Have I told you how pleased I am that you guys aren't going to add her to the hoard of people in the area with a *Max* in their names?"

"That was more at your brother's insistence than mine. Said he'd invent a new computer game or something to create our own legacy fund to save her the chore of being another Max Turner. I'm happy not to have to follow the tradition, because the only Max name I like, you've already got."

They rose to their feet and Maxy hugged her tight, kissing her cheek lightly before leading the way out of the Sugar Shack. "Give my love to Junior when you see him."

"I will."

A flash of regret stole over Tasha as she slipped into her car. Maxine had become a good friend, someone she trusted to have her best interests at heart. It still hurt not being able to share this kind of planning with Lila, who had totally cut her off, ignoring all attempts at contact, even leaving family events early to avoid her.

How could two people in the same basic family, Lila and Maxy, have such different approaches to life? Such different responses to her? Tasha thought about it the entire drive over to the house, and the only conclusion she came to was that whatever caused it, she sure liked Maxy's reaction better than Lila's.

Max stared at the computer screen unseeing for another

full minute before he gave up, rubbing his eyes and wandering out of the back bedroom. Complaining seemed foolish, but was it possible for him to stop getting additional business? He'd been inundated with new requests for both web designs and advertising proposals, and every one of them was a reference from someone he really shouldn't turn down.

The doorbell rang, and he hurried across the room to open the door.

"Maxy? Hey, what's up?" A quick check of his watch showed the entire afternoon had disappeared and he had only thirty minutes before he had to meet Tasha. He was still on a high from the whole time-to-call off-the-prenatal-rules event.

People who said guys couldn't get emotional needed their heads examined.

His sister slipped around him, pulling off her light jacket. "I need to talk to you. About important things."

He pointed to the living room and sat across from her. "Are these like business things, or should I be getting scared?"

Maxine's face flushed, and she fidgeted and wiggled like she was a little child waiting for their birthday cake to arrive. "Gramma wants to sell the house. She can't. There's no way she can let someone else have that place. It's way too important to the family, all that history and tradition tied up in the place and suddenly it's going to belong to strangers? I don't want that to—"

"Whoa, slow down. Who told you this? About her selling the house?"

"She did." Maxine stood and paced a few steps. "She said she's getting too old to take care of it by herself, and that she'd like to have regular company. She's been looking into a few of the local seniors housing that have room. If she puts up the house for sale and someone new buys it, all those years of tradition will be lost. We can't let that happen. What are we going to do?"

With every sentence her voice rose slightly higher. Max scrambled to calm her. He'd never seen his sister so agitated. "I thought that house was a part of the Turner Legacy. I'm sure of it, in fact."

She pulled to a sudden stop and whirled on him, her forehead creased with a frown. "What does that have to do with the legacy? I know we'll be getting money because of having the Max in our names, but the house?"

"The house is a part of it." He spoke quickly, rubbing her arms with his palms. "There was some kind of clause stating it can't be sold if there are Turners of age to inherit. I'm not exactly sure—it's a long time since I saw those papers, and I was pretty young back then. Let me go find out the details, but if I remember right, you, me and...Maximilian might be the ones eligible for inheriting."

She took a steadying breath. "Okay. I'm sorry. I would just hate to see that place not a part of the clan. But...how would that work if there are three of us to inherit? Are we supposed to all live in it together? That's not going to work."

Max pretended to think for a second, putting on a serious expression. "Well, it is a pretty big place. Tasha and I could take the main floor, you get the second, and we'll stick old Mill up in the attic rooms like a bat. He'd like that. Suits him too."

She stuck out her tongue at him and stepped away before giving him a sheepish smile. "Thanks for calming me down, but I'm still concerned."

"I promise to do what I can to make sure the house doesn't need to be sold." He thought about the mortgage he and Tasha had on the new house, and how little they actually owed due to her scrimping and his college windfall. His ability to make this work was far better than his sister knew, but he wasn't going to share that information until he'd had a chance to talk it over with Tasha. "We'll be able to figure it out."

Maxine nodded, then twisted her fingers together. "There is something else."

"Is this like...personal?" Her body language screamed it was personal.

"Sort of." She blinked up at him with her big innocent eyes. "How did you know you and Tasha were in love?"

Oh man. She was still seeing Jamie. Old Twinkle Toes hadn't gotten any better with time, not as far as he was concerned. "Are you asking because you think you might be in love?"

She shrugged. "I don't think I am, but I'm curious. Is it really something heart-pounding and unmistakable?"

"Hell, yeah." His instant response brought a chuckle from her, and as they laughed together, he scrambled to find the words that would both encourage her and discourage her from looking for love with the wrong guy, i.e. Jamie the wishy-washy. "It's not only heart-pounding, it's butterflies in the stomach and shivers up the spine."

"Sounds like a bad medical condition," she teased.

He thought about Tasha, and the way she was trying to open up and let him completely into her life. The last week had been different. That ghostly wall hadn't appeared even once, and everything in him wanted to jump up and down and rejoice. "Terminal, for sure."

Maxine rose and paced toward the windows, turning back slowly. "So, if there's nothing like fireworks, it's probably not love?"

He hated to say it, but he couldn't leave it at that. "Now

you're being silly. Even in romantic love there's more than the physical thrill. There's thinking about them all the time, and wanting the best for them. Wanting to be with them, like the way sitting in the same room as Tasha can make me happy. Are you telling me that you feel fireworks when you hug Gramma? Or Mom and Dad?"

"Of course not."

"But you love them, and me, and the cousins and the aunts and—"

She laughed. "Okay, enough. Yes, I love the whole lot of you. Some more than others, and you, only at times."

He winked. "You know what love is, sis. If you're looking for fireworks, you're probably asking about sex, and that's one discussion we are not having."

The instant flush over her cheeks was amusing. "No, I don't want to talk about sex with you. Don't worry."

"If you need to talk about that, chat with Tasha. Only make sure I'm working in a faraway place, and I'm wearing headphones." She wrinkled her nose, and he tweaked it with a laugh. "Hey, I need to go now, if I'm going to make my date with Tasha."

She smiled as she picked up her coat and headed for the door, him right on her heels. "I had coffee with her this morning. Things are going really well for you guys, aren't they?"

He nodded as they waited for the elevator. "It's been the most incredible year of my life."

"I always thought you guys would be good together. I'm glad." There was a little note of longing in her voice and he impulsively hugged her. He wanted to tell her to give it a while, but he knew what it felt like to be waiting for the right person.

Now if only Tasha would admit he was the one for her.

Chapter Seventeen

Max raced into the house and caught Tasha in the midst of flipping though a catalog with samples of door trim and floor moldings. He snuck behind her and circled her extended waist, pulling her back against him. "Well, hello, beautiful, fancy meeting you here."

She turned with a happy smile and kissed him sweetly. "You're right on time. I was about to flip a coin and make the rest of the decisions all at one shot."

He shrugged. "Sounds as good a way to decide as any." He dug into his pocket and pulled out a quarter, and offered it to her.

"Goof."

"At your service."

She raised a brow. "Promises, promises."

They walked through the house hand in hand, making the last-minute decisions listed for them in the folder. Maxwell's mind was only half on the task, and a lot more on everything else he'd had dropped on his lap in the last few hours.

"You okay? You seem distracted." Tasha nudged him as they moved back to the kitchen area. The cupboards were all hung, the island and countertops all in place. The only things missing were the appliances, the knobs on the doors, and the tile flooring. Max ran a hand over the shiny sinks as he considered what to say.

"Maxy was asking some pretty deep questions. I guess I'm thinking about them."

She nodded. "She told you too? That's good."

He frowned. "You knew about Gramma wanting to leave the house? How did you find out already?"

"Gramma Turner is leaving the house? That's sad. I'd hate to see the place no longer a part of the family."

"It should stay in— Wait, what were you talking about?" Confusion swirled in his brain. "If you didn't know about Gramma, then I don't understand. What did you think Maxy told me?"

She looked away, evading his gaze. "I don't know if I'm supposed to tell you."

"Tasha..."

"It's not my secret to share."

He pressed her back against the wall, trapping her with his arms on either side of her head. She grinned at him, the heavy swells of her breasts and belly bumping his body, and a shot of lust raced through him. "Do I need to torture it out of you?"

"Hey, if that turns your crank, I'm all for it." They leered at each other.

Max paused, his ache for her checked by his concern for his sister. "Is Maxy's secret something I need to worry about?"

Tasha shook her head. "She'll tell you when she's ready."

A rush of gratitude hit him. "You've become a good friend to her. Thank you."

That one brow went up again as she stared him down. "I'm not doing it for your sake. She's a great person."

"Still, I'm glad you two get along so well."

"Me too." Tasha dug her fingers into his hair and tugged his lips to hers. He got lost in the kiss until the rising sexual tension around them was broken by the enormous yawn that escaped her.

He nibbled on her neck. "Too tired to fool around?"

"Not really, but there's no bed here anymore. And I'm not doing it on the porch again. We actually have neighbors here, and no fence yet. So unless you have some other brilliant idea…"

Brilliant ideas? He had a million of them. A fair number of them involved that oversized Jacuzzi tub they'd had installed in the master en suite. He'd cleaned it up the other day to ensure the plumbing was hooked up correctly.

"What's that look for?" She waggled her brows.

Shit. "You mean my poker face wasn't doing its job?"

Hands tugged at his shirt, pulling his T-shirt free of his jeans. She slid her warm palms up his back. "Nope. And usually you're such a good player. Pity. I think I'm going to have to demand a payment for your lack of control."

"I thought you were tired." His hopes rose. While he loved the talking time, and planning and simply being with each other, he couldn't get enough of her. All the physical changes she was going through thrilled him, and while it would be fun when she wasn't pregnant to be able to get a little more athletic again, he wasn't complaining.

"I thought so too. It's not fair, you know, that you still manage to make me excited even when my brain wants nothing more than to shut down and hibernate."

She dragged her fingernails down his back, and he arched, groaning out his pleasure. "Shit, woman, I'm a caveman right now. It's not your brain I want to get intimate with."

He reached under the loose fabric of her maternity top and found her breasts. Her head fell back against the wall as he massaged gently, catching the tightening nipples under his thumbs in endless circles.

"You planning on sharing your brilliant idea with me soon? Because although I have some awesome memories of this wall, I somehow don't think my belly or my balance is going to cooperate enough to make this a viable spot for sex."

"Don't be in such a hurry, woman. I want to enjoy the appetizers out here, then move for the main course."

She laughed, the light sound breaking into a shaky moan as he pushed her top up and licked her nipple over the fabric of her bra. "As long as you're prepared for me to melt into a puddle of goo when you're done."

"Hmm." He tugged down her bra to reveal what he was searching for. "I like goo. Chocolate flavored? Strawberry?"

"Does sex have a flavor? Oh, yes."

He paused in the middle of twirling his tongue around one tight nipple. "You have a flavor. Kind of vanilla and maple at the same time."

She pulled him off one side and he willingly went to pay attention to the other lonely breast. "Are you calling me vanilla?"

"You? I highly doubt it." He closed his lips around the tip that beckoned to him and sucked in tiny pulses. Tasha's voice quivered as she moaned his name.

He teased her for the longest time, loving being able to share his desire like this. There was plenty of time to softly worship her breasts before running his hands up and down her inner thighs and over her ass.

Hmm, her ass. He rotated her to face the wall, then he knelt and pulled her hips backward slightly to rub his palms over the rounds. Hidden beneath the denim maternity pants, he couldn't do much more than squeeze and press in circles, dragging a hand down the seam separating one sweet cheek from the other.

Her muffled words snuck out from where she'd rested her face against her arms, leaning on the wall. "I know it's not kosher to say this, but I love it when you touch my ass."

He bit one cheek, enjoying the little moan that escaped her. "Who says it's not proper? I've told you myself. I love your ass. In fact, I'd like to fuck your ass."

A gasp escaped her as Max rose swiftly, fit the bulge of his jean-covered erection between her cheeks and rocked lightly. Waiting to see what she'd say.

It seemed as if Tasha was silent for a long time.

"You're serious?" Her voice carried a trace of lust.

Oh yeah. "It's completely safe while you're pregnant. I researched it online—"

"Oh God, I can just imagine what your search history looks like right now."

"I behaved, I only read the articles. Skipped the pictures and the videos." He nipped her earlobe. "Up to you, I've got the perfect location, and the position should feel real good."

As he waited for her response, he raced his hands over her body, savoring the way she moved against him. Seeking his touch, striving to keep him in close contact. She tilted her hips a couple times, easing his shaft along her crease and he smiled.

"Damn you for being a sex god, Maxwell Turner. Let's do it."

They slowly made their way across the house to the master

bedroom, articles of clothing falling aside in an abandoned mess. Every few steps he simply had to kiss her again, touch her. Taste her. When he finally took her into the bathroom and sat her on the raised ledge, stripping off her panties, his throat choked up with need. Her breasts were heavy, the areolas larger than before, the nipples themselves reacting quicker than usual to the light touch he drew down her torso in a wave. Her belly rounded in front of her as she sat with her legs demurely closed.

He stripped off the rest of his clothes and stepped into the tub, flipping on the water before suddenly realizing he needed one more thing. He squatted in front of her, his cock straining upward between his legs as he took her mouth in a brief, one-hundred-proof kiss.

"I'll be right back."

He leapt over the edge, ignoring the water he splashed on the plywood.

She called after him. "Nice ass yourself, by the way."

When he got back she'd slipped into the half-filled tub and was leaning back on the sloped side, one hand resting lightly on her belly.

The sight held him spellbound. Her lashes touched her cheeks, her face peaceful. All thoughts of sex were pushed aside with the need to care for her. He dropped the container he'd grabbed and crawled in slowly, stopping the taps and lifting her into his arms.

Her head rested against his shoulder and she made a happy noise.

Max smoothed a hand down her back, rubbing and caressing. It was the most frightening thing to hold his heart in his arms like that. Tasha and his child. He ignored the desire still coursing through his veins and simply appreciated the gift he'd been given.

Or at least he ignored it until Tasha reached out and wrapped her fingers around his erection. Any hardness he'd lost was quickly regained at her touch. Long smooth motions followed, her thumb slicking over the sensitive head until his balls tingled.

"I thought you'd decided to have a nap," he teased.

"Preserving my strength for the main event." She lifted her lips to his and they got lost for the next while. Kisses that involved tongues and teeth and lips. Wet brushes with fingers over slippery body parts, parts that drove Max crazy as he listened to the sounds of pleasure escaping her lips, bouncing off the walls.

The bathroom wasn't finished yet, the trim and the mirror missing. There was no towel rack, no ceiling-fan cover. No pictures on the walls, no candles or personal paraphernalia. Nothing to fancy up the place and say that this was their home.

But it *was* home. As each day passed and they spent more time planning the finishing touches, Max felt his soul slipping a little more into the house and changing the four walls to a haven.

Tasha twisted, attempting to straddle him, but he resisted, pulling her back into his lap instead with his shaft tight to her ass. "Oh no, you teased me enough. Now it's my turn to take control."

He nipped at her neck, holding her in place. She squirmed lightly and he paused, ready to set her free if she wished. Then he realized the minx was merely taunting him, rubbing hard against his cock with every movement.

"Shall I take that as your final answer?" he asked.

Tasha glanced at him over her shoulder, her eyes half-hidden behind secretive lashes. "Take me."

There wasn't an inch of skin on her body he hadn't touched. Max had primed her to such a point Tasha was sure she'd go off at the slightest brush of his fingers. When he opened the plug in the tub and let the water start draining, she wanted to protest. The warm liquid felt heavenly against her skin, supporting the extra weight she carried in her belly. He kissed her shoulder and leaned over her, reengaging the stopper and positioning her onto hands and knees. The water level was high enough her torso rested in the water, but low enough that when he pulled her hips, her ass was in the air.

She laughed. "Did you research this as well?"

"Nope." One hand rubbed her cheeks, trailing between her legs to pat her clit lightly, and she tightened, the sensation so damn good. "No research, just a bit of honest luck."

He rubbed and caressed, kissing her back, pressing his torso close to keep her warm even while he heated her sexually with barely any effort. The relentless touch of his hand triggered her first climax, gentle waves contracting inside as the water splashed around them.

One finger passed between her cheeks and she shuddered. She'd enjoyed anal sex the few times she'd done it with previous lovers, but she and Max had never gotten around to it. While she was trying to get pregnant it wasn't in the plan, then she'd been too sick or too tired. Anticipation rose, a tingling desire in her core. Max was very good at making everything else pleasurable for them both. Being with him physically—finding new ways to enjoy each other—that was as big a part of learning to trust as anything else, right?

When he grabbed a container from the floor, she had to tease. "Do I want to know why you have lube with you?"

"Hey, you're not always around, but the thought of you

always is. A guy's got to be prepared."

She closed her eyes, relaxing as he pressed in a single finger, gently working the lubricant deeper. Two fingers stretched her, then three. All the while he floated his other hand up to where her breasts hung, supported by the water. The deep need inside her grew as he fed the hunger with his caress until she shook. He removed his fingers and pressed the slick head of his cock against her.

Pressure, hard. Hot. Every inch burned with a delightful bite, nothing that she hadn't experienced before, nothing she wanted to deny herself now. It was strangely comforting—with no concern about hurting the baby, she was once again a sexual creature and not a mom-to-be.

"That is so damn sexy, seeing you take me," Max growled. His fingernails skittered over her cheeks as his groin rested tightly against her. She was full, completely stretched, a deep-seated necessity for...something...building rapidly.

"Move. Oh God, Max, move."

He pulled back slowly, his fingers digging into her skin where he clutched her hips. He stopped before he would have separated their bodies and rocked forward so slowly she felt every single nerve as if it were hit with an individual beam of pleasure. One stroke after another, each time deep and complete. His balls hit her sex, and the tingle spread from her ass to her core. She braced herself on one arm, adjusting until she could free her other hand. The water had cooled slightly around her, warmer sections swirling as she slipped her fingers back to make contact with her clit. A hint of mischief encouraged her to reach farther to stroke his balls as he advanced and retreated.

"Minx." He moaned, the sound loud and heavy in the room. Water swished, splashing against the sides of the tub with every movement.

Her arm lay tight against her belly, the awkward swell nearly forgotten until now as she took in all the sensual sensations—combined with the words from his lips as he praised her and turned up the heat. Max increased his momentum, enough that combined with the pressure on her clit, her orgasm triggered, her pussy and ass both squeezing tight, white-hot pleasure flamed. Delight raced over her, the adventure erotic and fulfilling at the same time.

Max shouted and shook, his hands quivering on her hips as he found his release.

It never got old, being with him. It was the only time she felt like they were completely and utterly worry-free. Their united future was easy to believe when they were tangled together in sexual satisfaction.

The edge of the tub was at the perfect height, and she rested her forehead on the smooth cool surface, waiting for the world to stop spinning.

Max took care of her. Washed her clean, cuddled her into a blanket even as he stood dripping.

"I'm sorry, I'm going to hide some towels and stuff here for any future...adventures."

His hands were tender as he helped her dress.

"Let me take you home," he whispered.

All through the blurry ride back to their apartment his words from so many months earlier echoed through her brain.

We are home.

Maybe. It was getting easier to believe.

Chapter Eighteen

"You nearly ready to go?" Tasha rounded the corner and stopped in dismay. He had all three of his linked computer screens active, and the entire surface of the desk covered with papers. "Max, we're supposed to be there in fifteen minutes."

"Damn. Just...give me a second." He peeled himself away from the computer, stripping off his T-shirt en route to the bathroom. Tasha stood in the doorway, adjusting her stance to let the weight of the baby sit somewhere other than against her bladder.

This kid was far too interested in dancing on that part of her anatomy when it was the most awkward.

"You okay on going out tonight?" she asked.

"Of course. I got distracted for a bit."

Tasha attempted to read his expression, wondering if it was her overactive imagination kicking in. Her old fears and worries were still too easily raised. She glanced at herself in the mirror. Three weeks to go until the baby arrived. While she'd managed to keep from gaining too much weight, she was certainly not a fit and fabulous twenty-something. Not even a fabulous thirty-year-old. She looked...pregnant. After a full day of work, and a few too many restless nights of sleep, she had begun to understand what the books and classes had warned about—losing energy for anything but the most basic of tasks.

She refused to slow down. Next week they got to move into their new house. There was so much to do to get ready, including the surprise she'd been keeping from him.

What if she curled up tonight with a book like she longed to? Maxwell would also ignore the summons from the family, and it would be another night of family activity he would have missed because of her.

Damn if she'd be the one to come between him and his family.

He soaked his entire head under the taps, popping up to rub his dark hair with a towel. The short strands stuck every direction and she smiled. Physically he was as intriguing to her as he'd been when they started this adventure. One more glance in the mirror, and doubt hit her hard. She was far more than the woman she'd been back then, and having him say he wanted this baby didn't mean he'd been prepared for the changes in her body.

The kiss he pressed on her cheek was rushed and brief, and a flutter of apprehension assaulted her. Freaking pregnancy hormones. Tasha didn't know if she was coming or going at times. Trying to figure out if she had a reason to be legitimately worried, or if it was just the pregnancy making her into a crazy woman was maddening. She kept it subdued on the ride over, not wanting to voice her concerns before what was supposed to be a fun and relaxing event.

They were only a few minutes late, and the teams hadn't been chosen yet.

"Dibs on Tasha and Junior," a couple of voices called simultaneously, laughter ringing through the room.

Max waved and bent to whisper in her ear. "I hope they know they're getting a pair of slightly sleepy teammates."

"Talk to your daughter," she whispered back.

They grinned at each other and she made another vow to try and trust that he'd keep loving her. First, she had to survive the night.

When they stopped the game for a stretch break, people scattered to grab snacks and drink refills. Tasha heaved herself vertical, Max at her side as always.

"You want an elevator to help you with that?" someone joked. She held back her retort, not sure how a *fuck off* would be received. Laughter rose and she turned to spot Max deliberately aiming his middle finger at the funnyman and she had to smile.

"I've asked Max to design a levitation system." More amusement surrounded them and he squeezed her fingers. There were times it was hard to remember people didn't really mean any harm, and a light joke carried the unintended hurt off quickly.

She hightailed it for the bathroom, or as fast as she could now that her pelvic floor seemed to be made up of all baby, with no room for her legs to swing. In spite of promising to maintain her "take it with a sense of humor" policy, if anyone said one word about waddling, heads were going to roll.

She slipped out the back door when she was done, staring into the green of the yard. Summer was attempting to take over completely from spring, with a freshness in the air that she'd longed for. Her internal heaters were set high enough to keep her, and Max, warmer than they liked most nights, but she loved this time of year. A pair of chairs tucked in the darkness beckoned, and she wandered slowly toward them, intending to sit and relax in the quiet for a bit.

Until she noticed one chair was already occupied. Lila stared at her in dismay before her expression wiped clean, her face blank.

Tasha swayed from foot to foot, uncertain what to do. Seeing her old friend was awkward, uncertain. She'd all but given up on her.

"You may as well sit down," Lila offered, bitterness tingeing her voice.

Uncomfortable. Edgy. The injustice of the situation swept up and surrounded her. They'd been such good friends before— at least Tasha thought they'd been. But good friends didn't completely stop talking to each other. Since that cutting conversation back before the wedding, she could count the number of words they'd exchanged on one hand. Her best friend had avoided her like the plague.

Did she want to sit down? Try to have a conversation and figure out why Lila had deserted her? There were nearly a year's worth of memories that had been lost between them. Sudden anger hit, a need to discover an explanation for the hurt Lila had caused. Tasha sat carefully, the wicker chair seeming too fragile to hold her and her precious cargo. When she finally settled she looked up to see Lila's gaze burning on her belly.

Tasha deliberately stared into the backyard, hoping that out there somewhere she'd find exactly what she needed to say. Did she tell Lila how much her rejection had hurt? The woman had to already know. Should she ask her why?

Did she really want an answer?

"I'm sorry. I didn't realize you and Max were going to be here. I would have stayed away." The ease with which Lila spoke made the lump in Tasha's throat seem baseless. Why was she hung up over something Lila had obviously already put behind her?

Because it was years of friendship? That streak of anger rose again.

"There are a lot of family events, Lila. It seems stupid that you're going out of your way to avoid us. In fact, I'll say it. The whole situation seems idiotic. I don't understand why you've gone and smacked me in the face like this. Why you put our friendship aside just because Maxwell and I got together."

"I don't need to justify myself to you."

Tasha sighed. "It's not asking for justification, it's asking for any reason that makes a lick of sense. If we'd done something to hurt you, I could see it, but it's like you flipped a switch. One minute we were friends, the next we weren't. Can't you see why I don't understand?"

Lila glared. "You want me to say something like I didn't approve of you two being together because I was concerned about the difference in your ages. I was *soooo* worried, because I know what it's like to have been in love with someone younger than me, and I know the terrible heartache when they decide to go back to girls their age."

Tasha stilled. The words were sarcastic, and over the top melodramatic—it was obvious Lila was being a shit. "But that's not the truth, is it?"

The other woman made a face. "Of course not. And it's not because I was worried about him hurting you, like those other jerks you'd dated who broke your heart. Even though I had to listen to you build your life up again, help convince you that you were a valuable person in spite of the shit your family led you to believe. It's not because I was worried that my friend had gone and seduced one of my younger cousins simply for the purpose of finally finding a decent guy."

The words slashed like knives, cutting into her soul. "Why are you acting like this? Are you sad I found someone to love and you didn't?" That was the only possible explanation Tasha had thought of.

"Oh, yeah, that must be it. I'm longing for a guy to come along and make me whole. I really want to get pregnant. I want someone who will be there to make me change my life to suit him, but when he decides he's had enough of playing grown-up, or when he decides that my body isn't beautiful enough anymore...he'll leave."

Bitterness poured from Lila along with a lack of understanding of what being with Max was like. There was a rotten taste in Tasha's mouth from simply listening to Lila spew her garbage.

If she could have risen from the chair dramatically she would have, but she was trapped. Instead, Tasha let the frustration she felt escape in her words.

"It's clear you don't want to share why you've written us off. I guess I should say thank you for avoiding me since you're not able to explain what's wrong. I wonder that you were ever really my friend since you threw it away so easily."

Lila laughed. Brittle, and harsh. "I have no idea why, but the thought of you two drives me mad. *Jesus*, Tasha, I don't understand it myself. I've tried to reason it out. Am I jealous? Am I upset that you seemed to give up all your vehemently sworn ideals in a flash? I don't know. Maybe you're right and we never were friends. All I know is that I've tried my damnedest, yet all I see when I look at the two of you is pain. Whether that's me projecting my failings on you, I don't know. It's just not worth it, okay? You go on with your life, and I'll go on with mine, and sometime I'll learn to be polite to you guys, but right now, I can't." She stood and walked away without another word, tearing apart the final threads of attachment that Tasha had still clung to even after all this time.

Tears fell. Tasha rocked in her chair, arms wrapped around her belly. She'd seen this coming. Hell, she'd thought she'd already given up on Lila, but having that last bit of hope torn from her burned. The refreshment of the evening retreated as misery filled her.

Those were acidic words that had been spoken, and she shouldn't listen to them. She knew that, knew better than to take to heart something meant to cut and rip. Still, the old fears snuck out from where she'd hidden them, to taunt her with their cruel bite.

Lila, who had been her friend, had left her. Completely. Unreasonably. It had to be her fault. There must be something intrinsically wrong with her that made people reject her.

Doubt and fear settled like a heavy black blanket, smothering her joy. She fought back, searching her memory for the truths she *should* cling to. Max had shown his love a million different ways. How could she not accept it? Take hold of it with both hands and let herself love him?

She willingly acknowledged he loved the baby. He cared so much for family, there was no way she could deny that, no matter what, Maxwell would be there for their child. He'd also said he loved her, but that was still much harder to believe, especially with Lila's fresh dismissal piercing her heart.

She wanted to believe. Wanted to love him back, but that last step was proving more than she could take. Call her a fool, say she was crazy, but even almost a year of being loved wasn't long enough to erase the pain of too much previous rejection.

The baby rolled, feet and elbows bulging the surface of her skin and she sniffed, running a hand over the thin layers separating them. This was the only truth she knew to be absolutely real. There was someone here who was going to need her and would accept her completely.

"Tasha, where are you?"

She wiped her eyes frantically as Maxwell stepped down the

porch toward her. "Here."

"I was worried. Not even you take that much time in the bathroom." The teasing tone in his voice matched his expression for a split second as he knelt beside her. Then he spotted her tears and swore. "Hey, what's up? You feeling okay?"

He dropped a hand to cover hers where it rested on her belly. She grabbed him by the back of the neck and pulled him close, burying her face in his neck. Leaning against his body in an attempt to draw strength from him. While the evening was tainted with the poison of Lila's words, she didn't want to make it worse by giving Max ammunition to want to hunt his cousin down.

The constant rubbing of his fingers along her neckline soothed her, but she'd had enough. "Just hormones. Can we go home?"

"Of course. I'll grab our things. You don't even have to come back into the house."

Yeah, that would be good to avoid. Having to explain that Lila had been cruel, or blaming the tears on the baby—neither of them sat right. He helped her up, his hands tender on her body as he brought her to the car and seated her.

"Let me say good night for us and I'll be right back." He raced up the stairs with his usual energy as she collapsed back in the seat, grateful to be away from the crowd and any reminders of the twisted conversation.

They couldn't go on this way. Somewhere she had to find the strength to take the final steps needed to rid herself of her fears.

Chapter Nineteen

"Wait a minute. Back up a bit. Did you crash or get a virus?"

"Neither, I think. But there's a whole section of the files I can't access anymore and I'm not sure why."

With that, Max's goals for the morning dashed out the window. He had to take this call—rescuing the program now was preferable to having to rewrite the entire system later. He scribbled a note for Tasha who was still asleep, and left.

It took nearly two full hours to rescue his client's computer, and since he was out, he stopped on the way back to pick up a few groceries and do a few chores.

Gramma had made the decision to move. He'd received the papers that he and Tasha needed to sign so Maxine could go ahead and take ownership of the Turner's legacy home. Miracle of miracles, their own house was done, with the first loads of boxes already taken over. Tomorrow the rest of the furniture would be moved via Turner Clan Express, and they'd officially start life in their new home. In the nick of time too, with the baby's due date only two weeks away. Fourteen days, or three hundred thirty-six hours, or twenty thousand one hundred sixty minutes...not that he was counting or anything.

Max yawned as he leaned back in the elevator and waited to reach their floor. Tasha was already looking ready to pop, and uncomfortable all the time. He slipped into the apartment, anticipating the day they'd be in the house and he wouldn't need to take that long trip anymore.

"Tasha? Where are you?"

He dropped the bags in the kitchen and went looking for her. It didn't take long—she had collapsed on the couch with her shoes kicked off and her eyes closed. Seeing the dark smudges under her eyes turned a knot inside him. Maybe it was a normal part of having a baby, but she seemed so tired all the time, especially since that game night a week ago. He'd even asked at the last prenatal visit if she might have caught something, but the doctor had laughed.

"It's called pregnancy. She'll get over it soon."

He sat beside her, wanting to smooth his knuckles against her cheek but resisting for fear he'd wake her. The mound of her belly lay on the couch next to her like an obedient puppy, and wonder of wonders, the baby fidgeted and he saw the movement.

Just a little longer and I get to see who you are.

"You were out for a while." She stared up at him, her eyes barely opened as she sighed drowsily.

"Work emergency. And groceries, and gas. Plus, I picked up the final light fixture the builder insisted they couldn't get. Idiots."

She frowned. "I'm sorry. I should have done those things, but I'm feeling awfully lazy."

He gave in to his need to touch her. He tucked his hand around her neck, leaning down to kiss her soft lips. "Please. You're not being lazy. I told you I'd do them, just wasn't expecting to do them this morning."

"What was the emergency?"

"Just computer stuff. Next time, though, I'll get Maxy to take the call. She's doing great." In fact, she was better than she thought she was. He'd have to remember to let her know.

"She's very happy working with you."

Her words pulled him back to attention. "And I'm glad to have her on board. I feel bad that I've loaded her down with a bunch of extra work over the next while."

Tasha stretched, reaching down to lift her belly with her hands as she twisted to a sitting position. "Don't worry about it. She needs something to distract her right now."

Max crawled up on the couch, settling her between his legs so he could reach around and massage her stomach. She moaned with pleasure, relaxing against him and his heart leapt. "Why does she need a distraction?"

"Why? She broke up with Jamie."

Hallelujah. "Finally. I mean, she never mentioned it to me."

Tasha snorted. "You really think she was going to with the attitude you've shown toward him since the start?"

"Good point. I'm still glad he's gone. She needs a far nicer guy."

She let her head fall back on his shoulder. "She doesn't need nice, Max. She needs someone to let her be herself. I just hope she..."

The words faded away and she attempted to retreat.

"Oh no, you don't." He scrambled around and blocked her path. "You don't start a sentence like that and then leave in mid-thought. You hope what?"

Tasha wrinkled her nose. "She's looking for her independence, that's all. I mean, she's the same age as you, and she's feeling the need to find someone to love. I think she was hoping Jamie would be the one. I don't think he was the right guy for her first."

"Argh." Max stood and paced away. "Thanks for sharing that with me. Damn it, why didn't I know they were getting that serious?"

"Umm, hello?" Tasha frowned. "She's old enough to know her own mind. It wasn't your job to be the defender of her virginity."

Max stopped in confusion. What was Tasha giving him hell for? Shit... Okay, not a topic he wanted to discuss. "No, I'm not talking about her having sex. I didn't expect her to be some kind of vestal virgin until she died, although I would have been happy to discover she was."

"Don't be a hypocrite, Max. You had sex before we got married. Hell, we had sex before we were married."

"I know, I know, but she's my..." Her glare stopped him cold. "Okay, I won't use that 'she's my sister' as an excuse again, but you know what I mean. My parents are never supposed to do it, neither is my sister. It's an unspoken rule."

She shook her head. "You're a nut."

He gave her a mock salute before worry forced his legs to move. How come he never saw this coming? "It's the other part that bothers me. You said she's looking for her independence? You don't think she's going to run out and find some guy to move in with? Shit. That's why she was asking me all those questions the other day. I should have known."

Tasha wiggled her way upright, frowning at him. "Now you're being a jackass. She's not stupid—that wouldn't be independence. Like she needs another bossy male organizing her life. You know, not everything is yours to fix, discuss or be responsible for."

"She's my sister."

"*Jesus.* Good job. You went all of thirty seconds without using that excuse. Yes, fine, she's your sister, and your business partner. So worry about those roles, instead of the stuff you're not in charge of."

Max shook his head vehemently. "You don't understand. I feel like I've been neglecting her. I should have noticed. Not to fix it for her, but to be there and offer support. I've always been there before, and I had no idea this was even going on. I feel like I missed the boat."

Tasha held out her hand and he took it, helping her off the couch. When she leaned against him, he automatically hugged her, sheltering and holding her close. His frustration didn't diminish, but it slid to a back burner. How could he stay on edge with her in his arms?

Her voice was soft, but clear. "Max, how many hours are there in a day? And how many of those hours do you spend doing things for other people? Dealing with emergencies, taking care of family? Then add the hours you've put into building your business."

He still could have done better. "I've always been able to do it all before."

"You've never been in *this* situation before. You've dealt with your education and moving out and living alone—I bet during each one of those seasons of your life you had different responsibilities, right?"

Fuck. No fair breaking out the logic. He couldn't fight logic. "I know where you're going with this, but that doesn't make it any better."

She grabbed his chin in her hands and squeezed. "It makes it real. You can't be everything to everyone. You've got a full-time job, you've got me and a baby about to arrive. Your life has changed, this is your new reality. Maxine is old enough she's not going to share everything with you anymore. She's thinking about the same kind of things you have. About establishing a family and moving to the next stage of her life. Don't you want that for her?"

"Of course."

"And since you're not spending all your time with her, that means she's got time to visit with others like me. I think she's enjoying my company. Are you going to begrudge me that?"

"Of course not."

She squeezed him hard, her smile lighting up her face, and she'd never looked more beautiful. "Then set the routines into place that will let you take care of what's really important—like you taught me back when we started exercising together. Take care of the things that are important, and that's all you can do. But, Max, make sure you're *asking* your sister what's significant to her. You might be surprised how eager she is to grasp more independence, especially from the family."

The sense in her words settled deep. "I still think Jamie was an asshole."

Tasha snickered. "Agreed. And I guess he sucked in the sack—"

"*Nooooo.*" Max slammed his hands over his ears and mock-glared at her.

She covered her mouth to hold back her laughter, the other hand dropping to support her belly.

Minx. He tweaked her nose, then more seriously wrapped his hand around the back of her neck, staring into her beautiful eyes. God, he loved her. "What would I do without you?"

He leaned in and kissed her thoroughly before grabbing a file folder off the table and retreating to his office. He needed to figure out the legalese of the family legacy and the house, so he could make sure that Maxine didn't lose the one thing she'd already made clear *was* important to her.

Tasha stared at his back as he left, feeling as if she'd somehow won the lottery. Being able to reassure *him*? Priceless.

She wandered into the kitchen, struck by a sudden desire for orange juice. After pouring it, the bags of groceries on the table caught her eye, and the dirty shelves in the fridge. They'd be moving tomorrow and the fridge was still a mess. She pulled everything off the top shelf, grabbed a warm washcloth and a small box, and started organizing items as she organized her thoughts.

This morning she'd woken with a million different threads running through her brain, looping around and knotting together until she'd given up on sleep and hauled her heavy body out of bed and into the shower. The water had done nothing to clear the tangled mess, and she'd wandered the apartment restlessly for hours.

The venomous night on the porch a week ago had become a catalyst in her life. She had seen it—there was something so bitter in her old friend that it had leached into her soul and now flooded out to hurt others. It hadn't been pretty to experience, but realizing that Lila dealt with that bitterness daily made Tasha more determined than ever to move on.

She didn't want to be like Lila. Bitter and alone. Refusing to accept the love being offered. Tasha was tired of being dragged back down by the things she'd thought were long buried. For the past week she'd been systematically going through all her emotional baggage. Stacking the items up and considering if they were worth holding on to, or ready for the trash.

Unfortunately, for every hurt she tossed aside, the pain of remembering took its toll and she'd been exhausted. Even this morning she'd finally admitted defeat and crawled onto the couch and collapsed with the chill of the past clinging to her.

Waking to look into his loving gaze.

Max.

He'd said he loved her. Shown it so many different ways. The thought he might not return her feelings, or might sometime choose his freedom over her—neither of those situations worried her anymore, no matter what Lila had said. Of the two of them, who should she believe? There was no contest. Maxwell Turner was a trustworthy man.

His concerned face from minutes earlier rose to her mind, and the flash of inspiration that hit made her grab the fridge door and cling tight. Right now, they were dealing with the same issue. The same advice she'd just given to Max applied to her.

Your life has changed, this is your new reality.

This was where she was—and the people she was with. She wasn't the child abandoned by a father or uncaring mother; there were no cheating partners or unfaithful friends in her immediate circle. She was a thirty-four-year-old woman with a baby on the way. There was a man in her life who loved her, and cared for her with more energy than any one person had a right to possess. She had true friends and family surrounding her who would do everything they could to make her happy.

They all loved her.

But most of all, there was Max.

Tasha wiped away the tears flooding her eyes. There was no more denying it—how much she loved him. It had taken far too long to admit it, but it was there, inside her.

No rockets went off, no loud thunderclaps or brilliant fanfare accompanied her realization. Only tightness in her throat, and a building joy to melt the final layers of icy fear that had coated her heart for so long.

She loved him.

In the middle of her apartment kitchen with the mismatched appliances and all the cupboard contents loaded into cardboard boxes, her world turned one hundred and eighty degrees. Her own little miracle, and not a single person witnessed it.

She marveled over her realization. Love—such an ordinary event, but oh-so-extraordinary as she acknowledged it for the first time.

Tasha leaned over, the skin on her stomach stretched taut, muscles aching slightly. She slipped the box onto the clean shelf and stood, hands tight to the small of her back.

The front muscle band across her stomach, way down low, tightened again and she groaned. Damn Braxton Hicks. Talk about the ordinary and the extraordinary combining. She'd been experiencing the false contractions off and on for the past three weeks. They weren't painful, more annoying, like a muscle that had been worked to the point of fatigue, tight and rigid. The first time they'd hit, she'd been astonished and slightly afraid. Now she took it in stride, breathing slowly until the muscles relaxed.

Again, awareness hit her. The reality was their baby would be here soon, and her body was getting ready. The practice contractions, as the books called them, were preparing her for when the real thing came along and Samantha would arrive.

Tasha had to laugh. Maybe if she considered all her waffling over the past months as practice loving for the real thing, she wouldn't regret that it had taken so long for her to admit her true emotions. Ignoring what she felt for Max was a lie she refused to continue to tell. She wanted all of him. Every bit of his heart and soul, and she wanted to give all of herself to him as well.

Tasha snuck to the door of the office and peered in, watching him work. His fingers flew over the keyboard as he spoke into his headset. This should be forever. Them as a family—no, as a couple first—without any doubts, any fears. The poison that Lila had flung had watered down to nothing, diluted by the depth of compassion and caring Max had shown for so long.

Thinking again of Lila caused the final piece of the puzzle to click into place. There would always be someone who wouldn't accept her unless she did what they wanted.

That wasn't love.

Max must have seen her in his peripheral vision because he turned and smiled, asking to be excused from the person on the line. He swung the mic away from his mouth and held a hand to her. She took it and shuffled forward into his embrace.

"You need me?" he asked, smoothing a hand over her cheek.

Oh my God, yes. "Always."

His grin widened. "I was planning on working for the afternoon to finish this up. You okay until supper?"

She nodded. Her heart was bursting to tell him what she'd realized, but even she, unromantic as she was, figured blurting out *I love you* right now wasn't the way to do it. "I'm pretty sure I can keep myself busy. I'll see you later."

He kissed her quickly, squeezed her fingers, then dove back into whatever he was doing.

The anticipation of being able to share with him gave her a burst of energy. Suddenly, it wasn't enough to wander the apartment dealing with the final packing details. Tasha checked her watch—there was more than enough time if she left immediately. She grabbed a sheet of paper and wrote him a note, left it on the table and headed out the door.

Chapter Twenty

It was hours later before he dragged himself from the computers. He'd constantly found that one more thing to complete, but the end result was a lot more productive than he'd hoped. With luck he'd be free for the next few weeks, giving him time to be there for Tasha. Settling into their new home, getting ready for the baby to arrive.

His phone rang, and he grabbed it, wandering back into the apartment to find Tasha and discuss supper plans.

"Junior, do you know where Gramma is?"

He chuckled. "Is this a trick question? Isn't she at the house?" He glanced around for Tasha—no sign. She must be in the bathroom.

"No, and we can't figure out where she's gone. After Tasha took her for the tour at the seniors home—"

"What?" He checked his watch. It wasn't just past supper, it was nearly eight, and the sun was approaching the horizon. "When did Tasha take her anywhere?"

"You didn't know? Gramma called to tell me she didn't need a ride because Tasha was there and would take her."

What the hell? His anger burst out at his sister. "And you didn't think that a eight-and-a-half-month pregnant woman might not be the best person to escort our eighty-year-old

Gramma around town?"

Maxy hesitated for a second. "I'm sorry, but honestly, no. It didn't occur to me. They're both very self-sufficient."

He spotted a piece of paper on the table and snatched it up. There were only two lines, nothing to indicate Tasha would be gone for a long period of time. Picking up a few things, stopping at the house site, that was all. Fear rolled over him. She should have been home long ago. Something must have happened. He raced to pull on his shoes.

"Shit—I need to try her cell phone. Call the nursing home and find out when they left." He hung up before Maxy could respond. Images of Tasha lying hurt at the house flashed through his mind, making him crazy.

Her line rang and went to message. He tried again.

Icy fear surrounded him. His heart was in his toes as he stabbed the button for the elevator repetitively, urging the damn thing to hurry up.

His cell phone rang with her tone, and he scrambled to answer it. "Are you okay?"

The line crackled, breaking up slightly. "We're...fine. We need help. Gramma Turner and I are a little...at the moment. We went...walk, and she's twisted... It's okay, but I can't..."

"Where are you?" Details later, location now.

"Cemetery. She wanted to..." The line went dead.

Screw the elevator. He was through the emergency exit and racing down the stairs before his call to Maxine even connected. "They're at the cemetery. Don't know why, but I'm heading over. Phone reception out there is almost impossible to get, so they could have been stuck for hours. Tasha said that Gramma's twisted something. Call a couple of the uncles to come help me."

Maxine's voice quavered a bit. "I will, and, Junior, I'm sorry. I didn't mean—"

Shit. "It's not your fault. You're right. They're independent, and stubborn, and there's nothing you could have done to stop them. Love you, sis. Call you when I can."

He drove well over the speed limit as he raced toward the family plot, cursing that he was almost twenty minutes away. The Turners had a whole damn section in the Thompson Cemetery, a fact that had fascinated him when he was little, but now seemed a trifle macabre. It was like the clan was still doing things together, even now that they were dead. He skidded to a stop, leapt from the car and raced toward the rise where Grandpa Turner was buried. The steep slope of the hillside cemetery suddenly seemed to have been laid out specifically to slow him in his quest to reach them. One final burst of energy and there they were, Tasha's dark head close to his Gramma's white one as they sat perched on a low wall. The only lighting in this section was a small decorative imitation gas lamp a good twenty feet away, casting a tiny glowing circle along the edge where the women rested.

"There he is." Gramma raised a hand and waved. "Over here."

Max slowed to a walk, eyeing Gramma quickly, then taking a more thorough examination of Tasha. "Ladies. You went for a very long stroll."

Gramma sighed. "Wasn't supposed to be that protracted, but silly me. I was trying to be frivolous and now my ankle's not cooperating."

He laid a hand briefly on Tasha's knee as he squatted, taking his Gramma's ankle and checking it carefully.

"Ouch. Yes, that's the part that hurts. I need someone to lean on, and Tasha and I decided she probably wasn't the best choice to use as a crutch right now."

Thank God. That's all they would have needed was for Tasha to lose her balance and the two of them end up hurt. "Good thinking. Lean on me, I'll get you back to the car."

Gramma hopped down, and he wrapped an arm around her. He offered his other hand to Tasha.

She shook her head and waved him on. "I'll wait. You take Gramma, then come back for me."

He didn't like that idea, not one bit. Before he could argue Tasha visibly winced and he stared at her, trying to figure out why— *Oh my God.* He might be exceedingly bright, but this was something he'd never experienced before. "Tasha?"

She covered her lips with a finger and tilted her head toward his Gramma. "You two go ahead. I'll be fine for another few minutes."

No. He was not leaving his wife in a graveyard, in the dark, when she obviously was in labor. Gramma would understand...and then he saw the dilemma.

There was no good solution.

He held out his hand to Tasha and she smiled at him, squeezing his fingers tight.

A shout in the distance made his heart leap as one of his uncles arrived, and he gratefully passed Gramma over with a whisper to his uncle to have an ambulance sent.

Tasha winked at him, then tucked her fingers under her belly and rubbed. An instant later he had her enfolded in his arms, his hands supporting her belly.

"You...martyr. What happened?" He helped her up and she let out a whoosh of air.

"There was something I wanted to talk to her about, and then after we'd already visited for an hour, she asked if I'd drive her to the seniors home. There was nothing wrong with that, but the next thing I know she'd convinced me to come and visit... Oh, hang it." Tasha bent slightly, hands on her knees, her breath escaping in rapid gasps. Far too rapid.

He rubbed her back, feeling more than a little helpless. "Hey, remember our classes. Slower, if you can. You've got a long time to—"

"Maxwell, I've been in labor for the past three hours, I think I've figured out the damn breathing bit. My water broke just after we got to the graveside and I sat down intending to call you. But reception sucks, and then your Gramma took a step the wrong direction and...oh my God, this baby is on the way."

This was not at all how she'd planned her afternoon to go. It was supposed to have been a short, simple trip. She'd be back in plenty of time to drag Max from his work and slather him with kisses before making her big announcement that she loved him silly. Tasha waited out another set of contractions, staring at the greenery around her as it faded into invisibility, the bright dashes of color muted as darkness settled. The other part of her brain worked hard to ignore the fact that unless an ambulance showed up soon, *very* soon, she just might have this baby in a graveyard.

It was sure to be one of those stories that down the road the kid would love to share with everyone.

Max supported her, touching her gently, rubbing and asking how he could help.

The comfort of his presence made a world of difference. "Just hold me. I'm so glad you made it. I didn't think your Gramma wanted to be a baby catcher."

"Why you didn't tell her you were in labor?"

Tasha took another slow step, his arms around her torso. "I

215

didn't feel anything unusual at first. It's only gotten bad since I got hold of you. I thought it was more Braxton Hicks, and I didn't think Gramma needed something else to worry about."

Max swore, holding her carefully, guiding them down the rocky path. "On the relative scale of things to worry about, going into labor trumps a twisted ankle."

Tasha shrugged. "I guess. Oh damn. Fuck, fuck, *fuck*, that one hurt." She stopped again, trying to catch her breath, but it was a struggle. In the far distance, the siren of an ambulance cut through the air. The pain shifted, and suddenly instead of squeezing her to pieces, a sharp pressure speared between her legs. "Umm, Max?"

He ducked in front of her, staring up into her eyes. His face was white in the pale light, and he looked far older than usual. "What?"

"I need to push." And like right now. She might want to wait, but this kid had other ideas.

"Shit, are you sure?"

She snapped at him. "No, it's just a sudden fancy I have. Arghh, crap, this hurts. It didn't so much...*shit*...until now, but... Oh my God."

"Okay, okay, let me..." He looked around frantically while she bit the inside of her cheek hard enough to draw blood. Oh yes, there was something going on, and the men with the nice flashing lights and blaring siren racing toward them might not make it in time. Maxwell ripped off his shirt, laid it on the ground and carefully helped her down on top of it.

"Another one of your school shirts bites the dust," she teased.

He lowered her pants, hands gentle on her body. "How can you joke right now?"

She wasn't sure. "It's joking or screaming. Which would you—?"

The pain struck the words from her mouth and Max scrambled to finish undressing her, her pants getting caught on her shoes until he tore them off her feet.

This wasn't how they'd pictured it. There was no sterile birthing room with a shower and tub to relax in while they waited for the little one to arrive. Of course, if Tasha was honest, she'd never thought *too* hard about the messier parts of the process, skipping straight from announcing "I think it's time" to "It's a girl" in one smooth blend like a television-friendly soundtrack-filled sitcom.

She might have made a detailed list of what she wanted, what she didn't want, but she'd never actually considered how much it would hurt, especially as all of her chosen cocktails were denied her. She'd briefly debated having a natural birth, but this—this was going too far.

"I can see the top of her head. She's got fuzzy hair. Okay, this is actually very cool." Maxwell looked up from where he knelt between her legs, his smile shaky. They had one hand joined, her fingers crushing his as she fought the pain. It wasn't the most elegant of locations, with her head resting on the grass, the dark shapes of tombstones casting shadows around them.

She didn't give a damn where they were anymore.

"Can I push?" *Oh please, sweet baby Jesus, let me push.*

"I think so. Not too hard." He pulled his hand from hers to touch her carefully, a light stroke over her burning skin. "This is her head pushing against you. You need to go slow—"

"Dammit, Max—"

"Stop. Not so hard. Hit me later, but you've got to slow down, slow...oh shit, yeah."

The cries escaping from her throat blended with shouts from the parking lot. Bodies surrounded them as the paramedic team arrived. Latex-gloved professional medical attendants raced up, white smears against the darkness around them. She wasn't sure what she expected. The pain was focused enough as it gripped her she just wanted this over and done, and she didn't care who pulled the kid out. It was in an almost dreamlike state that she noticed one of them squatting beside Max.

And Samantha arrived.

The pain washed away in seconds, mysteriously leaving nothing but the ecstasy of seeing their little girl held in her husband's arms. Her heart pounded loud enough she was sure everyone heard it. Then everything blurred together. All through getting cleaned up and transferred to the stretcher. The entire time it took to bring her to the ambulance and tuck the three of them in for the trip to the hospital—she saw nothing but her daughter, now cradled in her arms. The perfect gift, with her hair still wet. Little lips puckering into a bow and pulsing together, looking for something.

Maxwell opened her shirt and helped her bring the baby to her breast and it wasn't sexual, but it was the most intimate of moments. Her eyes were so full of tears she could barely see him not a foot away from her.

His one hand rested on the baby, the other behind her head along the back of the stretcher. Protecting and guarding them both, and the love inside him blazed out like a beacon.

It didn't matter what nasty things other people had said over the years, or the misunderstandings of her youth. What was real was now. What was true was this. She looked down at the baby once more, shocked to find such perfection in her arms, and yet what else could she have expected?

It was perfect love that had made her.

She reached for Max, sniffing back the tears. Whispering softly into his ear, for him alone.

"I love you."

He sucked in a quick breath at her words, the fingers cupping the back of her head shaking slightly as he kept their cheeks tight together.

She had to finish. Had to make it clear she wasn't just dropping platitudes in a flush of excitement. "There is nothing I want more than to have you and this little one in my life, and whatever else our family becomes. But it starts with you."

He didn't speak for a second, but she felt the brush of his lashes against her skin, wet with emotion. "I love you so much."

They sat and stared at the miracle in her arms while the miracle in her heart finished its magic.

Chapter Twenty-One

"Are you serious? A blindfold?" He stared at it with suspicion.

"Hey, I'm the boss of this. You want your surprise, you wear the blindfold."

Max shrugged. He stopped en route to kiss Samantha who lay sleeping in her bassinette. He grabbed the baby monitor, clicked it on and stuck it in his back pocket. "Fine, but there's something about closing my eyes that makes me very nervous."

"Hmm, you like it when I ask you to close your eyes." The lusty sound in Tasha's voice infused a little extra life into his groin, but he was too tired to follow up right now. Maybe when Sam started sleeping better—hopefully before she turned twenty.

Thinking back over the past weeks made Max grin. While Samantha's early appearance had been unexpected, her dramatic entrance had ushered in only the start of the celebration.

Tasha loved him. She'd accepted his love, and turned around and poured herself back into him ten-fold. It was like she couldn't stop saying it, or showing it. The woman he'd fallen in love with so long ago had not only arrived, she'd arrived in style and was a willing participant in every single moment they spent together.

The wait for her to come to terms with her past had been tortuous, but she seemed to be making up for lost time. The intelligent, funny and caring woman he'd always seen had an extra twist to her smile when she looked at him these days, and he planned to enjoy it.

Especially if it involved blindfolds.

He let Tasha lead him through the house, the floor plan automatically scrolling through his mind. "If you plan to toss me off the back deck, aim me in the direction of the compost pile. That would be a soft place to rest."

"Do we need to get a dog so you can have a doghouse to sleep in?" she teased.

He slipped the hand that rested on her shoulder lower until it covered her breast. "I'd much rather sleep with you. Even if all we do right now is sleep." What he wouldn't give for a solid eight hours. At seven weeks, Samantha was a good baby, but she still had her days and nights mixed up.

Tasha twisted under his hands, rotating in a circle. He brought his other arm up to embrace her, savoring the fullness of her breasts, lowering his grip as she continued to turn. He smoothed his palms over her slimming waist and firm ass. He enjoyed touching her body, but even better was having her playful and flirty again. Last week they'd made love for the first time since Sam's arrival, and other than going slow at first, Tasha had been fully online.

"I have no idea what you're doing, but it's totally working for me."

She laughed. "I planned on spinning you in circles to get you disorientated, but maybe a little distraction will work just as well. You know where we are in the house?"

"Who cares?" He caught her against him, cupping her butt firmly and dragging her up his body. Perhaps he wasn't too tired after all. Warm, soft lips met his, and he shuffled backward until he felt something solid against his back. One twirl placed her between his body and the wall as he ravished her mouth.

Okay, he was definitely not too tired anymore. The constant rhythm of Samantha's breathing sounded through the baby monitor and while she slept, he wanted to play.

Tasha scratched his back and bit his lower lip, sucking it into her mouth hard before releasing it with a smack of her own lips.

"Hmm, this is fun, but it's not what I had in mind."

She wiggled and Max reluctantly lowered her feet to the floor. "Rain check?"

Her fingers threaded through his as she tugged him forward again. "Definitely. And can we talk about your tendency to pin me against walls? I'm not sure when you picked up the habit..."

He could picture the smirk on her face. The tone of her voice revealed her amusement, and her delight in being with him.

There was no doubt anymore. They were in love—they were *both* in love—and it was so good. That cloud hovering over them had dissipated and while he imagined they would still have their struggles, right now things were pretty damn perfect.

Well, nothing that a good night's sleep wouldn't fix, anyway.

She pulled him to a stop and pressed against him, the swells of her breasts brushing his chest as she kissed him quickly, then undid the blindfold. She stepped aside and he swore softly.

"The secret room? You're finally letting me look in the

secret room?" The off-limits area had been driving him nuts since the midway point of the construction project. He had no idea what the space was to be used for, and any teasing attempts on his part to find out had been waved off.

"It's time. You ready?"

She twisted the knob and pushed the door open, letting him enter first.

It was an office. Natural light poured in, but the computer desk sat in such a way to allow a monitor to be easily visible. Shelving and storage lined one wall, a comfy chair—one of his favorites from back at the cottage before they'd moved in together—tucked into the corner of the space with a small coffee table next to it.

The desk itself was larger than the foldout table he'd been using in the makeshift space he'd set up back at the apartment. Way roomier than the corner he currently had his things wedged into in the office he was sharing with Tasha, one door farther down the hall. There was more than enough room here for all his monitors and screens, but for now, the only thing resting on the smooth surface was a picture they'd taken of the three of them—Samantha in Tasha's arms, him holding them both.

"It's beautiful, Tasha." He paused. "Is it for me?"

"Of course it is." She grinned at him.

Minx. "You had me believing we were going to keep sharing office space, or that I was going to have to find another spot in the house to work."

"I thought the suggestion for you to work at the kitchen island was my best—you know, so you could do all the cooking as well as your designing."

Max stepped up to the window and peered out. The space they'd set aside to build a playhouse for Samantha was directly in his line of vision. He turned back to Tasha. "I love it. It's perfect, but where did you get my chair? I thought we'd gotten rid of it when I moved in with you."

She grinned. "Remember I went to go see your Gramma the day I went into labor? I was sure she'd taken some of your things, and I wanted her to save that chair for me."

He laughed. "You're kidding. That's the big secret reason you went over there? You're a nut."

"I guess the nesting instinct hits me harder than most."

Two steps brought her back in his arms. "It means a ton that you arranged this for me."

She slipped against him tight, burying herself against his chest. "I wanted a way to prove to you that I...want you around. All the time. That you belong in my life." Her voice skipped for a second, and he lifted her chin, surprised to see tears in her eyes.

"Tasha?"

"It's okay, it's just that..." She wiped her eyes quickly. "There's more to our relationship than being friends. Or being lovers. I understand better now that it's going to take work, even if everything goes well."

Max nodded. "Family is work, but it's worth it." He stopped in confusion. "When did you have time to put this together? I know it's not since Sam was born. Or, I don't think so, unless I've been sleeping harder than I thought."

"I made my first plans after we saw the ultrasound. It would have been done weeks ago if Sam hadn't arrived early. Since then it's been tough finding the time and energy to complete everything, and I had to work when you were out."

He tweaked her nose. "You were supposed to be resting."

"I was, that's why it took so long. A task takes forever to

finish when you only put in five minutes at a time. I had the idea earlier, but I was scared to start anything until then."

Before she'd admitted she loved him, she'd already been building him room in her life that proved she wanted him around. That meant something. Something good.

He kissed her, holding the sides of her face in his palms tenderly. His lips and hers together, gentle and yet needy at the same time. She lit a fire in his body that was ready to flare up at any moment, but the steady burn of the flame in his heart was even more powerful.

When she pulled away, he complained.

"You're not done looking." She pointed at the door in the sidewall.

"I thought that was a closet."

"Nope."

He pushed the door open and laughed. She'd somehow turned the walk-in closet into a tiny boardroom. There was the most gorgeous solid wood table with four leather chairs. A floor-to-ceiling window looked out on the backyard, and he realized he'd never noticed it from the outside—a pile of extra sheets of plywood had been hiding it from him for months. He turned on her.

"You crazy woman. You had this planned to the last detail, didn't you?"

Tasha smiled. "You need a place to meet clients, and down the road, so do I. This space is big enough for me to spread out blueprints, and you and Maxy can fit with at least a couple of clients if you feel you need a more formal setting than a coffee shop."

"So that leads to the office I've been using?" He pointed across the room and she went and unlocked the door, opening to the familiar sight of his desk and equipment.

"I stole the closets from both rooms to get enough space, which is why we need all the extra shelving. We'll have to coordinate so we don't have people booked for meetings at the same time."

Max laughed. "I think we can manage that."

Her hand brushed softly along his arm, fingers caressing up his biceps until she reached his shoulder. "I didn't get everything set up. Figured you'd want to arrange it to your liking. And I didn't think we should try to keep sharing one office once I start taking on contracts again—I was warned by a fair number of people that was a plan for disaster."

It almost slipped past him. *No way.* "Other people knew about this?"

"A few." She grinned, and he shook his head.

"You do realize that at the next Turner get-together I will be teased unmercifully about being the last to know?"

"Ah-huh."

Her mischievous expression was going to get her in trouble. Right about now, actually. He pulled the baby monitor from his back pocket and examined it carefully. Hallelujah, Samantha was still sleeping. He placed it carefully on the floor by the door and turned to stare at his wife.

The bright happiness shining on her face made all the waiting worthwhile. So did the widening of her eyes as he stalked across the room and scooped her up.

"Max! What are you doing?"

He plopped her on the table, pushed her knees apart and inserted himself between her thighs. "Christening the boardroom."

Tasha fisted his shirt and met his lips eagerly. They were

co-conspirators, trying for a moment's connection before the reality of parenthood intruded again. Time was a precious commodity, and they laughed together, fumbling to loosen buttons, unzip zippers. They continued to devour each other, tongues edging their passion upward as they stripped away layers. He resettled her bare butt on the tabletop. Her hands snuck around his shaft, delivering long, smooth strokes with her strong fingers that brought him to full arousal in seconds. He dipped his head to tease along her collarbone lightly with his tongue, dropping his hand between her legs to stroke gently. She shivered under his touch, hips rocking in time with his probing.

Tasha's touch was so intoxicating he had to pull away before he ended up spraying across the new tabletop. She dragged him closer, aiming his shaft at her sex, but he had another idea.

It *looked* like a sturdy-enough table. Only one way to know for sure.

Max pushed her farther toward the center and prowled over top, pinning her to the warm wooden surface with his body. Skin to skin, so alluring, so erotic.

He wanted to touch every inch of her again. Take the time to tease and tickle his way down to the sweetness between her legs then back up once she'd come a few times.

A few soft gurgles rose from the baby monitor and Tasha swore. She wrapped her thighs around him and canted her hips.

"Screw the rest of the foreplay, I'm ready."

Thank God. He dropped to his elbows, kissed her passionately, and adjusted his hips until her heat engulfed him. Their bodies slipped together with an ease that sent a thrill up his spine. Familiar, and yet still so new.

The sun shone through the window to bathe them in its warmth as he rocked into her, the table solid underneath, the peaceful noises of their baby as she stirred creating the sweetest background. Tasha dug her heels into his butt, her fingers clutching his shoulders hard, panting moans of pleasure released against his lips as he unwaveringly maintained a steady tempo. For that single moment, time seemed suspended as they reveled in each other's bodies, in the connection between them. In the firm foundation they'd built their relationship on. He changed the angle of his thrusts, and Tasha gasped in delight. Her passage tightened around him, head lolling back as she came, his name on her lips. One final stroke and he joined her, jettisoning deep into her welcoming core.

They lay tangled together for another moment, hearts pounding, blood rushing.

"You know I'll never be able to have a meeting in here now without remembering this," Tasha complained.

He grinned down at her. "That was the idea."

As far as he was concerned, the memory-making would continue for the rest of their lives.

About the Author

Vivian Arend has hiked, biked, skied and paddled her way around most of North America and parts of Europe. Throughout all the wandering in the wilderness, stories have been planted and they are bursting out in vivid colour. Paranormal, twisted fairytales, red-hot contemporaries—the genres are all over.

Between times of living with no running water, she home schools her teenaged children and tries to keep up with her husband—the instigator of most of the wilderness adventures.

She loves to hear from readers: vivarend@gmail.com. You can also drop by www.vivianarend.com for more information on what is coming next.

Pushing the sensual limits can set off all kinds of alarms...

Turn It On

© *2010 Vivian Arend*

Turner Twins, Book 1

Inheriting her grandmother's home is a dream come true for web designer Maxine Turner. She's looking forward to a little freedom from the constant demands of her beloved, crazy mob of a family. When vandals expose just how vulnerable she is living alone, she seeks help.

Ryan Claymore's well-thought-out life was wrenched out from under him when responsibility for his special-needs stepbrother landed on his shoulders. Going from military man to business man hasn't been easy. He counts himself lucky he's found Maxine to trade his security-system knowledge for her website expertise.

The red-hot chemistry that sizzles between them comes from out of the blue, and they both fight a losing battle to resist. Even the secret Ryan hides isn't enough to keep Maxine from working her way into his heart—and his bed.

But something else might tear them apart. Whoever seems determined to destroy her home, and her sanity along with it.

Warning: Realistic multiple orgasm sex scenes, men getting in touch with their emotions, brothers being—well—brothers, and a very tempting back-porch swing...you have been warned.

Available now in ebook and print from Samhain Publishing.

HOT STUFF

Discover Samhain!

CPSIA information can be obtained at www.ICGtesting.com
Printed in the USA
BVOW02s0348200715

409480BV00001B/106/P